BLACKMAILED BY
THE BEAST

GEORGIA LE CARRE

You can discover more information about Georgia Le Carre and future
releases here.

https://www.facebook.com/georgia.lecarre
https://twitter.com/georgiaLeCarre
http://www.goodreads.com/GeorgiaLeCarre
978-1-910575-79-6

❀ Created with Vellum

CHELSEA

https://www.youtube.com/watch?v=0-7IHOXkiV8

"Oh, Father tell me, do we get what we deserve?"

"Ms. Appleby."

The busy street below my window suddenly ceases to exist. I freeze, not daring to even take a breath.

Thorne Blackmore?

No. No. No. It can't be. He couldn't have found me here.

And yet … I would recognize that voice anywhere. Husky and beautiful. I hear the click of my office door closing and his footsteps come closer. Closer still. So close I can feel the heat from his body. The raw power of his energy surrounds me and makes my skin tingle. In the industry they call him The Beast, because he is so cold and ruthless, his methods are pitiless.

"Hello, Chelsea," he whispers in my ear. The familiar rumble of his voice is bittersweet. Greedily, I drag in the scent of his aftershave, leather, pine forests, and the tangy ocean. I shut my eyes. Oh, sweet Jesus. How I have missed him. These last two years without seeing him have been hell. How did I survive? I walked wounded and bewildered. Days passed, then weeks, the leaves changed, the cold winds came, then the mornings began to fill with sunlight again. After the first year, I lied to myself. I told myself I had forgotten him. But like a ghost, this man haunted me.

Will he still match the memory I keep deep in my heart?

I take a step forward, then turn around to face him. For a second my whole body goes cold. It is like coming home to find that a leopard has leapt in through your kitchen window and it is eating your sweet little dog. He's standing there in his usual ten-thousand dollar suit and thousand dollar tie, but he is bulkier, deadlier, bloodier, scarier and; oh God, his eyes. The gray orbs were never warm before, but now they are as frozen as the most inhospitable winter lake. And yet he is *beautiful*. Beautiful like lightning ripping through the night sky, or the angry sea crashing into cliffs. The breath I was unconsciously holding escapes in a rush, and I stand there like a deer, beyond conscious control, motionless, sniffing the air, terrified, ready to run.

He studies me expressionlessly.

For a few seconds, I can do nothing but stare into those pitiless eyes. Then I force a bright, happy smile onto my face. *Pretend, Chelsea. You can do this. Just pretend.* "Hiya. What a lovely surprise to see you again." My voice sounds breathy and shaky.

He smiles slowly. A cold, mocking smile. Undertones of danger.

Oh, Mother of God. I decide to take the bull by the horns. "I know you must be angry, I'm really sorry I stole from you."

His smile grows. It could be mistaken for an almost friendly grin except for the hostile wasteland in his eyes. "Are you now?" he murmurs.

"Yes, yes, I am very, very sorry. It was a mistake. I shouldn't have done it. I'll make immediate arrangements to return the money to you."

His blunt charcoal eyelashes sweep down, and I stare at him hungrily. I never expected to see him again. He is spectacularly elusive. Even catching a glimpse of him is hard. He *is* hard. "What kind of arrangements might they be?"

"I … I have some savings and I'll take a loan for the rest and pay it all back."

"All of it?"

"Every last cent."

"With interest?'

"Of course," I agree instantly, even though I feel my stomach tighten. I probably won't be able to afford it, but maybe I can make a deal to pay him back monthly, or something.

His eyes glitter. "And the cost of finding you? Will you pay that back too?"

"The cost of finding me?" I repeat stupidly.

"Yes, it is very, very difficult to find a girl who stops using her credit cards, social media, and completely drops off the face of the earth."

"Well, living in New York is not exactly dropping off the face of the earth."

"Let's just say it is hard to find someone when you're looking for Chelsea Appleby, and she is living under the name of Alison Mountbatten, and has gone to considerable trouble to erase her digital footprint from the net. Didn't you ever miss going to your favorite online store to get those black shoes you love so much or that peach lipstick you always wear?"

My mouth feels like it's full of dust. I swallow hard. "Well, yes. However, I figured a new life was the best way forward."

"Hmmm ..."

"Look, you can either tell me now, or let me know later how much I owe you. I'll make the arrangements straight away. But I ... er ... have a pile of work to finish right now." I wave my hand in the direction of my desk.

"Um ... I suppose we could call it two million even."

My eyes pop wide open. "What? You can't be serious! You want two million? I stol ... took $300,000."

He shrugs carelessly. "Interest ... opportunity costs."

"Interest ... opportunity costs?" I echo incredulously.

"Three hundred thousand in my hands has unlimited investment potential," he sneers.

I frown. Thorne is so freaking rich he can give away three hundred thousand dollars without batting an eyelid. This is the man who flies hand-churned butter from France to wherever he is in the world. Three hundred thousand is a drop in the ocean to him. "Why? Why are you doing this? You don't even need it. All those billions sitting in your bank account. You couldn't spend it even if you tried. You don't even care about it. They're just numbers to you."

He takes his phone out of his expensive camel coat. "It's the principle."

"It's nothing to you. It's less than the cost of a round-trip in your private plane."

He lets his eyes flick to the phone in his hand. "But if you'd rather I alert the proper authorities instead—"

Panic surges through my veins. I raise my hand up. "Wait. Just wait a second. We can work something out. I'll pay it all back. I swear. I will. I just need a bit of time."

"So you can run away." His voice is icy.

"I won't run." Taking a rasping breath, I stare into his cold, watching eyes. "I promise."

He takes a step closer and I stop breathing. His hand rises up and he runs his finger down my exposed throat. "So soft and pale," he murmurs as his thumb caresses the skin where a pulse is kicking. "How can I trust a thief and a liar?"

"I give you my word," I choke out.

He shakes his head slowly. "No, Chelsea. Your word is not good enough. It was once, but not anymore."

To my horror my eyes fill with tears. When I blink, they spill down my cheeks. He laughs. "The oldest trick in the book, Chelsea. I should have known you'd stoop to that. Well, I'm afraid female tears have the opposite effect on me." He bends his head and licks my cheek, his tongue warm and velvety. He lifts his head and meets my stunned eyes. "They excite me. You, my little thief, are going to cry for me. A lot."

I did not realize that my hands had flown up. I must have wanted to shove him away, but they are resting on his chest, my fingers spread out on the hard muscles. "What do you want from me?" I whisper hoarsely.

"I want you to pay your debt with your body."

I hear my blood rushing in my ears, and I stare at him in shock. "What do you mean?"

"For three months, you will be my toy. You will sleep when I tell you to sleep, you will eat when I tell you to eat, and when I tell you to spread your legs, your only thought will be, how wide. During that season when you will be mine, I will use you when, where, and how I decide."

"You can't do that to me," I gasp.

"Or you can go to prison. You will be very sweet meat in a women's prison. All this soft, unmarked flesh."

I shudder and he smiles. "Yes, Chelsea, shudder you should. Trust me, my cock would be infinitely better."

"You could have any woman. Why are you doing this?"

"Because I can. Now strip."

THORNE

I stare at her beautiful eyes flashing with defiance. Two years I looked for her. All those long lens photos are nothing to seeing her in the flesh again. Her skin is so fine and pale. It is almost translucent. I never knew why they called it an English rose complexion, until I saw hers. It was the first thing I noticed about her when she arrived for her interview. My office is grey marble and chrome. Against that backdrop, she looked almost unreal. She had a distant smile that had my cock rock hard. Hell, I nearly didn't hire her that day. I knew she would be too distracting.

But I couldn't let a slip of an English girl throw me off my fucking stride. I had to prove to myself that she was nothing but a raw call to the flesh. That I was greater than the lust I felt for her.

Hiring her has been the most unprofessional thing I've ever done in my life, because from that moment, when I hired her, I never again had a moment's peace.

I plan to put a stop to all that frustration today. When I'm through with her I'll feel nothing but contempt. She is a beautifully packaged liar and thief.

"So the world famous AI inventor and bitcoin billionaire, Thorne Blackmore, gets his kicks out of forcing a woman to have sex with him," my little rebel taunts.

I laugh softly. She's so going to end up slung over my knees, and I am going to enjoy taming this little spitfire. Just the thought of reddening her saucy ass has me instantly hard. "No, not any woman, just those that dare steal from me. Now fucking strip before you try my patience."

Her chest rises and falls quickly as she weighs her options. Not many. Her eyes dart around the room. Thinking. Thinking hard.

She licks her lips nervously. "Look, this is my work place. I'll do whatever you want me to do, but … not here. Please. This is my livelihood." She looks at me, her wide, clear eyes pleading. "I don't want to lose this job. Please. After your three months are over I still need this job."

I stare at her. To be honest I'm slightly disappointed. I expected something more original. I guess I must have built her up in my mind in the last two years. I should be glad. I'm not in the market for a wife. I plan to discard her after I'm done with her.

"Please. Anyone could come in. Please."

"I locked the door," I murmur, and watch her squirm. She really has the most beautiful eyes. Green with molten gold flecks. Like precious jewels. I watch her pupils grow large and fuck if I don't want to bury my cock in her. This woman has been a thorn in my side from the day she

arrived. I must have her. Until then there will be no satisfaction.

She bites her bottom lip, and fuck if I don't want a taste. "I'll
go with you without making a fuss. Just don't make me do
this here. Please," she pleads.

I do the thing she does not expect. "Fine. Come on then."

Something flashes across her face. She thinks she has won. "I
have to put in the paperwork to ask for time off. What about
if we agree to a meeting place and I join you later and—"

She must think I'm stupid. "You are already on vacation."

She frowns. "What do you mean?"

I shrug. "Brian Harrington owes me a favor. I called it in. He
gave you the next three months off starting from fifteen
minutes ago."

Her jaw drops. "What? You spoke to my boss! What did you
tell him?"

"The truth. We had unfinished business."

Her shoulders slump and a heavy sigh escapes her lips. She
looks at me with a defeated expression. "All right. Will you
give me a few minutes to pack up some of my stuff? I'll meet
you downstairs at reception."

Her eyes are downcast and for a second I experience a
strange emotion.

Not pity.

Not empathy.

It's an odd thing. I've never felt it before. I try to pinpoint the feeling, but I can't. Then it hits me. I *have* felt this before. Never for a human being and not since I became an adult. I feel protective. It's the way I felt about my puppy when the silly thing injured itself and whimpered with pain.

This is not good. I turn away from her, not wanting her to see the expression on my face. "All right, I will wait for you at reception. Do not be long."

"I won't," she promises.

CHELSEA

T he door closes behind him. Minutes, I have only
minutes.

Not enough time. Think, Chelsea. Think.

Right, there is no longer anything for me here. I won't be
able to come back to this job, or this life again. This is the
moment I've always dreaded, and it's just as fearful as it is in
my dreams. When you're a thief, you live on that gleaming
knife edge. When you're a thief, you've planned your escape.

I pull the bug-out bag from my bottom drawer. The idea
came from an article I read written by an ex-Navy Seal. He
always had a bug-out bag filled with the essentials he would
need on a moment's notice. Grab your bug-out bag and go.
Mine doesn't include ammo and an automatic with silencer.
Mine is simpler, more civilian. It has a fake passport, a
burner phone, and credit cards with my fake name on it.

I've disappeared before. I can do it again.

From the canvas bag, I pull out a pair of faded blue jeans, the type of nondescript hoodie worn by your average convenience store robber, and a pair of running shoes. Transformations come in many sizes and hues. I slip out of my clothes and heels quickly and get into my escape gear. I try to do up the laces, but my hands are shaking so much, I end up tucking them into the sides of my shoes. I remove the crab clip that's been holding up my long brown hair, and the silky strands cascade down my face and shoulders. Pinning up my hair, I grab the dirty-blonde wig and fit it on my head.

I stuff my suit, blouse, and purse into the bug-out bag, and sling it over my shoulder. Slide on a pair of sunglasses, and look around my office. All the photos of my 'significant other' are fake. I take one last look at the little plant I have so lovingly watered. Like everything in my life it is expendable. Let it go, I tell myself. I will get another plant. Exactly like this. Somebody else will take care of this one.

I can go now. There is not one person I need to say goodbye to. There is nothing left here for me. There never was.

I open the door to quickly check the hallway. There's no one around so I step outside and close the door behind me. Hanging my head down, I walk as fast as I can towards the elevator. I call it and keep my head down. Karen from Audit passes behind me, but in my wig and hoodie disguise, she doesn't give me a second glance. The elevator arrives and I walk inside. The doors swish shut and I am alone.

As the elevator makes its quick descent to the ground floor, I pull a stick of gum from my bag and stuff it into my mouth to complete my image. I'm a full 180 degrees away from the uptight accountant I was just minutes ago.

Now, I'm the girl with a tax problem because I never

reported the tips I got while working at the diner. Like the government needs my paltry dimes. I try to remember the twang I should use if someone asks me a question.

The doors open with a ping.

As I step off the elevator, I spot the two large suited men by the entrance. I'll be damned if I get this far only to be caught by a pair of goons. Even after two years I recognize them. They are his men. They've been sent here to keep an eye on me in case I do exactly what I'm attempting to do now. Fortunately for me, they're looking for a dark-haired accountant in a conservative dark suit so, I have the advantage. I spotted them first so I drop my head and take a left.

Rule two of a bug out—always have an alternative escape route.

I move with a nonchalant gait towards the back entrance. I make it seem as if it is the most normal thing for a hoodie to belong in that polished space. By a fluke of luck, I just narrowly manage not to run head-on into Sienna, one of the secretaries. A wig and a hoodie would not have fooled her. I drop down and pretend to fiddle with my shoes until she passes.

Pumped up with adrenaline, I get across the lobby and start walking towards the janitor's room. If anyone recognizes me here it is not too dire. I'm good friends with all the cleaners. But I meet no one. Ahead is the door into the alleyway. I'm so close I can almost taste freedom. My heart is beating like an African drum as I open the door.

I can't believe it.

I'm out!

Then ...

Two massive men in dark suits appear at the end of the alley-way. They plant their feet shoulder-width apart and keep their arms relaxed by their sides of their bodies. Without any expression they stare at me. Why do these types always wear sunglasses?

I know I can run faster than them so I spin around and get ready to run like the criminal I am, but a black stretch limo rounds the corner slowly like an ocean liner. Long, blacked out, it's the equivalent of a hearse, and for me, it means a fate worse than death. My heart sinks. I cannot spend three months with the man. It broke my heart to steal from him. It will torture me to be with him.

I stare at the car stupidly as it comes to a smooth stop a few yards in front of me. It's so brand new it almost doesn't look real. His driver gets out and without looking at me goes to open the rear door. Then he stands next to it expectantly, saying nothing, just waiting.

What choice do I have but to brazen this thing out?

There will be other escape opportunities, I tell myself. I take a tentative step towards the car. My mind is a big fat blank. There is not one coherent thought in it. I walk slowly to try to stall for as long as I can. The closer I get to the car the more desperate I become. Like a trapped rat clawing and biting at the steel cage.

I reach the open door and pause. Only the lower half of him is visible. I note his trousers and his shoes. The best wool, the best tailor, the best leather. Other than the perfectly sharp middle creases on his trousers there is not a single mark or wrinkle on them. His shoes shine like a mirror. It is just like looking at an airbrushed picture in a glossy magazine. Unreal.

None of this is real.

It can't be.

With my heart crashing in my chest, I lean down. This is my moment of truth.

"Get in," he says curtly.

CHELSEA

I climb into his car and the driver closes the door. The sound is just a soft click, but it makes me jump. Now I know for certain. I can no longer fool myself. There will be no escape. There is nowhere to run or hide. I have to repay my debt. It is either submit to him for three months, or find myself in prison for years. Looking at his coldly furious expression, I know without any doubt that he will make sure that it will be the latter if I ever try to run from him again.

I slump against the seat. My breath comes out in a long sigh. It feels as if I have been holding this breath in for two years. I have been running so long I am almost at peace knowing I've been caught. There'll be no more looking over my shoulder for this cold, ruthless man; or running away from him in my dreams. I turn to look at him.

In the dimness of the car his eyes glitter like they are reflections of billowing smoke on glass. He's livid. I wonder if he's been angry these past two years. I pull my purse closer towards me; as if unconsciously shielding myself from his gaze. He snaps his fingers, and my eyes flicker towards the glass partition smoothly moving upwards.

"Where did you get that god-awful wig?"

Surprised, I touch my wig.

"Take it off," he orders.

I drag it off my head and hold it in my hands.

"Were you running away from me … again?" he asks. His voice is cool and calm; almost pleasant. It makes my heart beat even faster. I don't remember him ever sounding this way. For a man with such burning intensity, the sweet almost amused way he is speaking is unsettling.

I shake my head automatically.

"I told you I'd be waiting for you at the front of the building. Yet here you are, appearing from the back entrance."

I know that he's never liked being taken for a fool. Continuing this lie would be pointless, especially since it's pretty obvious exactly what I was up to.

"I'm really sorry," I whisper.

"Are you really, little Chelsea?"

I bite my lower lip.

His gaze dips down to my mouth before rising up to meet my eyes. He raises one thick eyebrow. "Perhaps you enjoy annoying me."

I shake my head. "No."

He looks at me curiously. "Were you trying to provoke me into punishing you?"

"I wasn't," I gasp, my fingers clutching my wig.

Thorne appears to lose interest in the conversation. He taps a button and the limousine purrs to life. The car moves forward as if it is floating on air. I study him intensely so that I can be a step ahead of him if I need to be, noticing every movement his body makes. He turns his face towards me, jaw clenched.

"Come here, Chelsea," he commands. His words are like ice and the hairs on my neck stand on end.

Unsure what to do, I lick my lips nervously. I hate to admit it, but mixed in with fear is pure excitement. No one makes me feel like he does. When he walks into a room the very air crackles with electricity and anticipation.

From the first moment I saw him, I wanted him with a clawing need. I lusted for the feel of his lips on my throat. I hungered for him to open my legs and take what he wanted. As time went on and he looked at me with nothing but cold professionalism I *needed* to completely submit to him, but always the burning intensity of my craving scared the shite out of me. I thought I could tame the desire. After I left, I thought it would go away with time, but no, it's just become worse and worse.

No matter what I did or where I went the lust for him never went away. I thought of him every day and dreamed of him at night. Sometimes, like a drug addict, I gave in and searched the net for stories of him. There was almost never anything. Why would there be? I knew what he was like.

He locked himself away in his high security home, building his AI. The only thing I gleaned about him was his AI was due for an unveiling in two days at a secret location in London.

All the invited guests were told only to keep the morning of that date free. The location would only be revealed individually to them, the time set to coincide with exactly how long it would take them to reach the secret location from their addresses. I knew all of London was abuzz. Those that received an invitation have cancelled all their plans in anticipation. This reveal is supposed to change everything in robotics.

"Why?" I whisper now, staring into those mysterious, unknowable alligator eyes.

"Come ... here ..." he repeats, a slight edge to his voice.

My dark past rises up, and I don't want to obey. I have worked so hard to make sure I'll never be in a position of helplessness again, but another part of me, a secret part, wants—no, wants is far too weak a word—hungers to submit to him. And that makes me afraid of him. I'm terrified he has the power to unhinge me. To callously undo the carefully painted mask I show to the world.

"Thorne, please..."

"I'm not going to ask again." His voice is cold and clipped.

My heart starts racing. Every self-preservation instinct in me kicks back. My hands clench to stop myself from lashing out, but I agreed to this. If I am to survive intact I have to learn to save my energy, keep the soft core of myself hidden. Fighting him every step of the way would eventually expose me. *I can do this and still stay strong. I am strong. It will take more than him to make me fall apart.*

CHELSEA

https://www.youtube.com/watch?v=JF8BRvqGCNs
(Stay)

I take a deep breath and scoot a couple of inches closer to him.

He reaches out his powerful hand and holds it a few inches away from me. I look at it, then his expressionless face, and back to his hand. Gingerly, I move my hand towards his, unsure of what to expect.

The moment my fingertips reach his palm, fast as a knife-cut, he grabs hold of my hand, and yanks me towards him. I collapse over his lap. Except for the horrified gasp that escapes my lips, I'm too stunned to speak. The smell of the luxurious leather upholstery fills my nostrils and I can feel the hard muscles of his thighs under me.

I don't struggle. I don't do anything. I can't. I just remain frozen and wait.

Thorne slips a hand under me and opens the closure of my jeans and pulls down the zip. Yanking my jeans down to my thighs, he rests a hand on my ass. Embarrassment floods my body. Why did I choose today to wear a black thong?

"Mmm…"

The hum makes me shudder. When he lays his large palm on my ass, I can't help my entire body from clenching or my nipples from swelling and hardening.

"You're far too nervous. Relax," he murmurs soothingly as he tightens his grasp around my waist and runs the fingers of his other hand along the bare skin of my bottom. One of his thick fingers slowly slips in between my legs. For heart-stopping seconds, he feels around the silky, wet folds for my clit. I grit my teeth and don't allow myself to moan with pleasure at the exquisite sensation.

As quickly as the touching begins, it ends. His hand is suddenly gone. When it comes back down on my flesh it is with such force that the crack reverberates around the interior of the car.

I scream out in shock at the intense burst of pain. I try to wriggle out of his grip but his hold is like steel.

"You … will … obey … me … Chelsea Appleby," he says, biting the words out with each new burning slap. Hot tears roll down my face and I have to bite down on my lip to prevent myself from crying out.

It is the most humiliating thing possible. To have a man punishing me like a naughty child, but a tiny knot is forming in my stomach, making me tremble with an aching perverse craving.

I never thought it, but it turns me on to know that his driver is on the other side of the partition and could possibly be hearing every sound Thorne's hand makes on my ass. I like the idea that I can cry out for help at any time, but I don't want to. He lands another blow, and I feel the vibration of it between my legs. My ass is on fire, but it is a pain that is mixed with an achy, illicit pleasure. In fact, I am shocked by how much the pain electrifies my pleasure. Each sensation working off the other. My sex begins to throb harder and harder with every blow. It's building into a crescendo.

I want him to reach for my clit again.

When he angles his hand, the next blow lands on my pussy. I gasp for air. Just as my pussy is dripping and I almost climax, he stops. He stops and gently tugs my jeans up. Thorne pulls me upright and sets me down next to him. I'm too afraid to look in his eyes. Too afraid to let him know how close I was to having an orgasm by what he just did to me.

Thorne reaches out to me, this time he is reaching for my face. I try not to flinch and keep my eyes on him as his hand brushes against my cheek. His touch makes me shiver. Then he slips his hand behind my head, and pulls my face right up to his so that I cannot avert my eyes even if I want to.

His face is more wildly beautiful than I remember. With his raven colored hair falling across his forehead, and his steely eyes like the ashy remnants of a fire, I begin to melt inside. My eyes travel down the strong, masculine bones of his cheeks, his proud Roman nose, and his jaw.

"Do not disobey me again, Chelsea. The next time I will not

be so kind." He breathes the words right into my face. They send a chill down my spine. Looking straight into his eyes, I search for his weakness. He cannot be so cold and cruel. He is not one of the AIs he builds. There must be some human emotion in him.

He pulls away from me suddenly and removes his grip from the back of my neck, but his touch lingers long after he has moved his hand away. I am still reeling by the way he had decided to punish me, and the way he claimed complete ownership of me.

The only response I can give is to summon up a wave of fury and hatred towards him and glare at him. I will never let him think I feel anything but disgust for him. I will not allow him to destroy me. I cannot let him see or touch the vulnerable soft spot that I have spent my whole life hiding.

I sit on my burning bottom a foot away from him and stare out of the window, frustrated not to have been allowed to come, and shocked that I had come so close to climax while he was punishing me.

CHELSEA

Many hours later, Thorne is still sitting next to me, but we are in a different limousine with a different driver, and in a different country. I look out of the window as we navigate through the streets of London.

I was born in a farmhouse in France, but I was raised right here, in the inner-city of London. I watch the people going about their business and feel a strange sense of disconnect. I never belonged in New York, but I don't belong here either. I really believed I would only ever come back here for one thing, but here I am, with only the clothes on my back.

Thorne drove me back to my apartment so I could pick up my passport. I don't even know why I bothered to ask if it would be possible to go up to my apartment alone. His dark eyebrows came together in a forbidding line and his nostrils flared with impatience, but the truth was I was not intending to defy him again. I already knew it would be pointless to run.

I just wanted a moment on my own. I felt so vulnerable, so

exposed. My thighs were wet and I wanted to change my underwear. Even more important I didn't want him in my tiny studio-apartment. I want to hide as much of myself from him as I can.

"Take only your passport. Everything else you need will be provided," he reminded me as we walked to the elevator.

I nodded, and after that no more words were exchanged. When I put my key into the door and pushed it open, he followed me in. His powerful presence filled the whole space. My apartment felt like a coffin. While his laser sharp eyes snaked around his surroundings coldly, I used the bathroom. My underwear and jeans were soaked through so I changed into a skirt. After getting my passport from the cupboard, I followed him out, putting my fate in his hands.

Now, as we pass Earl's Court, my eyes are drawn to the road that leads to my mother's home and a sad sigh escapes me. I feel Thorne lift his gaze from his laptop to look at me, unblinking and curious.

Instantly, I regret the slip.

I need to keep my wits about me, but unwittingly my eyes stray to his hand resting lightly on the corded muscles of his thigh. Without meaning to, my mind replays the sting of his slaps and the sounds I made, which I have since realized sounded more like moans of pleasure rather than protests, and that is probably what they were. It must be obvious to him as it is to me that the spanking he administered deeply excited me.

A fiery blush of shame creeps up my throat, and the upward curl of his mouth tells me he knows what I am thinking. I turn away in confusion to face the window again.

I really don't understand why my thoughts keep obsessively taking me back to that undignified time he had me sprawled across his lap. Especially since I'm actually frigid. I've had two boyfriends in my life and both have flung that word at me when I was breaking up with them. One in vicious anger, and the other with despair and a plea I get help for my 'problem'. I suppose I can't blame them; the sex was terrible. Both times and not because of them. Barry was quite good-looking and very attentive. He tried really hard to turn me on. He would have done anything I wanted, but there was nothing I wanted. Steve was a babe magnet. Girls just flew to him like moths to a lamp, but when we got down to sex, I just didn't want it. Nothing. Not the kissing. Not the touching and definitely not the actual sex. Ugh. Which is why my thoughts about Thorne are so confusing.

"Where are we going?" I ask, watching our reflections in the tinted glass window.

"Breckland House."

I whirl my head around in surprise. During the entire time I worked for him he never invited anybody to his house in Richmond. In fact, it is well known that he guards his privacy like the dragon guarding its lair. With complete and relentless dedication. No intrusions are tolerated. Ever. I've even heard that drones fly around his grounds twenty-four seven looking for intruders and paparazzi.

"I thought we would be living in your apartment in London."

His eyes spear me, half-exasperated, half-amused. "No. I have work to do."

I feel myself squirm and fidget like a child. "Oh, okay."

He turns away then and looks out of his side of the window. My gaze fixes on the thick black hair at the back of his head, and I wonder how it would feel to claw my fingers into it. When it hits me where my mind has slipped off to, again, I jerk my head around to face the scenery outside. I try to make sense of why he would take me to Richmond and not keep me in London. Why let me in?

At Hammersmith we turn off before we hit the motorway. After about twenty minutes we go past Richmond town. A few minutes later we turn off the dual carriageway onto a small road. Already I can see the property's high brick walls.

My mouth opens in a soft gasp when the car slows down, and the dark partition glass descends. In front of us are tall iron gates with golden lions stationed on either side. The driveway is so long that all I can see is land stretching on either side of us dotted with ancient trees. The house is so far from the gate I have yet to actually see it.

I look around in amazement. A herd of deer are grazing in the distance as the car slowly makes its way through the stunning grounds. When my dazed eyes meet Thorne's, I find him watching me, his expression veiled and secretive.

"This is all yours?" I ask in awe.

"It's my home," he says simply.

I nod. I haven't seen the house, but I know that it will be massive and austere. Just like his office, his car, his driver, his men, and him.

Even knowing that doesn't stop my mouth from hanging open with astonishment. What I'm staring at isn't a house at all; it's a vast mansion made from grey stone. Six Corinthian pillars soar upwards to bear an impressive plinth upon which is a statue of a bearded man in a chariot drawn by six white horses. There is a thick giant wooden front door and hundreds of tall windows with intricately carved stonework around them.

Thorne and I step out of the limousine, my legs are numb, my feet feel like clay. The car moves away, and I want to run after it. I'm terrified. Not of the house, or Thorne, but of me. How will I survive in these surroundings? I bite my lip. My chest fills with emotions I have no names for.

I gaze in awe at the large classical fountain directly in front of the house. It is a copper statue of a mermaid surrounded by strange creatures holding little jugs and pots spewing water into a deep pool teeming with big, brightly colored fish. It is the middle of winter. They must keep the water warm for the fish.

A tall man, with thinning white hair, wearing an immaculate black suit, and a middle-aged woman in a formal uniform, are waiting for us at the shallow stone steps. They make a small bow in our direction. Thorne introduces them as his butler, James and housekeeper, Anabel. He introduces me as Miss Appleby.

James's expression remains inscrutable, fatalistic even. His smile is polite, but not friendly. I recognize it because that is my smile too. I see in him a kindred spirit. Anabel is a different kettle of fish. She is about 20 years older than me. She cannot hide the deep curiosity in her watery blue eyes. Her cheeks are rosy and her smile, wide and genuine. I smile back at her. I've half-forgotten how kind the world can be.

It is cold, but Thorne removes his jacket. I try to avoid

looking at him. My eyes swivel around and I try to look past him, but I can't. I don't want to think about why I can't. One moment I'm fighting myself, the next I'm drinking his profile in. My breath catches. His hair is tousled, his eyes are hooded, and his skin is pale from all the hours he spends locked away building his AI. He is an impossibly beautiful creature. He hands his jacket to his butler who takes it so smoothly, it's like a choreographed dance move, or a slick calligraphic scrawl.

It's been a long time since I've seen Thorne in his shirt. I stare at him. There is something so wild and untamed about him. He is an enigma, unlike any other man I have ever met, both in appearance and presence.

His thick muscled shoulders, like those of a prize pitbull, are incredible, irresistible, as if he has been pulled from a story about shapeshifting men. He addresses his butler. "I'll be working in the dungeon, bring me a sandwich in an hour." He throws a glance at his housekeeper. "Show Miss Appleby to the blue room."

"Of course, Mr. Blackmore."

Without looking at me again, he turns at the hallway, and walks down a tall corridor full of tapestries to the west of the house. Interesting. He works in the dungeon of the house.

"Are your bags still in the car, lass?" Anabel asks.

I turn to face her. Her lovely broad accent tells me that she must come from North Yorkshire or somewhere close to it.

"Nope. I just have this," I say, holding up my purse.

"That's not a concern, your room has been fully stocked with everything you could possibly require during your stay here, but if there is anything specific you want, Ryland, the gardener, or even one of the other staff can nip into town and pick it up for you."

"Thank you."

"Come on sweetheart, I'll show you to your room."

As we walk up to the grand entranceway I have to drop my head back to look up at the majestic ceilings. They are all elaborately carved and look like they could have belonged to the palace in Versailles.

It is an absolutely beautiful house. Every artifact and art piece looks as if it was specifically designed to fit in this space. The curving stairs are a work of art. Made of beautiful dark wood with intricate gold banisters.

Anabel ascends the stairs and looks back briefly to make sure that I am still following her. I am only two steps behind. I run my hand along the wood, marveling at how deliciously cool and smooth it is. We make our way to the top of the stairs, then turn off down a corridor with a blue and pink runner carpet. Anabel stops in front of a tall door with a brass handle, before opening it and walking in ahead of me.

"This will be your room, Miss," she announces in the stillness of a large room.

CHELSEA

I stand at the doorway, astounded. The walls are papered with gorgeous gold-sheen Chinoiserie depicting vintage roses and beautiful birds. A massive four-poster bed is at one end. The bedspread is a mixture of teal, turquoise, and deep forest green. The floor is a dark wood, with an antique cream and emerald carpet. There is very little furniture, but each piece looks like it was bought at an auction at Christies.

From the tall windows one can see the front garden of the house. The opulent brocade curtains are held back with thick ropes of piled yarns twisted together. One of the windows has been opened a crack and a cool breeze rustles the long bullion fringes of the curtains, making the silky cords shimmer in the afternoon light. On the ground, they puddle into a soft meringue of exquisite color. A peppery smell mixed in with the sweet scent of potpourri catches my nose.

It is so beautiful it almost feels like being in a dream, an ephemeral fantasy world; but I feel stricken, filled with apprehension. To step inside this splendid room will be to enter my cage.

"Come on in, lass and I'll show you how everything works," Anabel invites, looking at me with open speculation now.

I look at her ruddy face. I have nothing to fear. There is nothing particularly malevolent about Thorne or this place. It is just my overactive imagination. I straighten my spine and square my shoulders. "What is behind those doors?" I ask, taking two steps into the room, and pointing to the three tall doors leading away from the room.

Anabel motions to each one as she explains their uses. "That door is your walk-in closet, lass. There are some clothes there for you and you can get anything else you want over the next few days. The second one is your bathroom. And that last door is … Mr. Thorne's bedroom."

I feel my cheeks flush with scorching heat. I didn't think he would be this close. The house is so incredibly large he could have put me in any room that he wanted. He must want to keep a close eye on me. "Right," I say briskly, to cover my embarrassment.

"Let me show you how the shower works, lass," Anabel croons, and starts walking towards the second door.

"Thank you," I say, when she has shown me how the heater and shower work.

"Supper, which will be served in the dining room, is at six o'clock. I will send Theresa, the maid, up to escort you down at quarter to. If you'd like a sandwich or a snack before that, just ring that bell, and I'll be more than happy to sort something out for you."

I want to hug her. She is so kind to a complete stranger. Thanks to her warm, caring face I feel far less anxious now than when I arrived at the house. I thank her, and she leaves, closing the door behind her.

Jet lag is starting to kick in and the bed looks more comfortable to me than I want to admit, but I decide to take a shower. First though, I give in to curiosity and take a look in the closet. I'll need something appropriate for dinner.

The 'closet' is almost the size of the bedroom. The floors in here are covered in a plush cream carpet. The walls are lined from ceiling to floor with shoes and clothes. Clothes that I have never seen before. In the center of the room is a comfortable couch, an armchair, and a dressing table.

I run my hands along the coats to my right and look down at the shoes underneath. The clothes and shoes have been coordinated by color and type. Next to the coats are sweaters and jackets, beside them are evening gowns, next to them, dresses, and it continues like this to the very end. Each item of clothing starts dark and gently changes to lighter hues. Whoever arranged these clothes must be very meticulous. I have an idea it is not Anabel.

I take a pair of shoes and sit down on the cream armchair to try them on. They are Christian Louboutins; pointed black pumps with red soles. They fit perfectly. I look all around and discover that every shoe is in my size. I step out of the Louboutins and walk barefoot on the soft carpet. I take a dress from a rack and hold it up. It is also in my size. I look around me in surprise. Thorne bought all these expensive designer things for me. I wonder how he even knew my size. Did his investigators go through my things in my apartment? Then an even more curious question. How is all this a punishment for stealing? A shiver runs through me at the thought of what is really expected of me.

I am just about to explore some more when I notice a turquoise rotary telephone on the coffee table. I pick it up. There is a dial tone.

I turn the dial to a telephone number that I have had memorized for years. It rings three times before there is an answer.

"*Hello?*" a cautious voice answers.

"Hello, Melody," I say, happy to hear the bubbly voice of my childhood friend.

"Chelsea is that you? My, what a surprise," she exclaims with a little giggle. "It says number unavailable. Where are you calling me from? And what time is it over there now?"

It is unusual for me to call her on the telephone. Normally, I would send her a text, or we would have a face to face chat on Skype or something, but calling her from an unavailable number never happens. "I'm in London, Melly," I say with a laugh.

There's a long, stunned pause on the other end. When I left London two years ago, I swore I wouldn't be coming back for a long, long time. Not unless I had to, and we both knew what I meant by that.

"What are you doing here?" she asks. There is deep curiosity mingled with fear in her voice.

"Thorne found me," I whisper. I don't know if there are hidden cameras or if Thorne is watching my every move.

"What? How?" Melly screams in a high-pitched shriek.

"Private investigators. Obviously, I was not as careful as I thought I was. He turned up at my office and gave me an ultimatum. It was either come back to London with him or go to prison."

"Wow! Since you're not rotting behind bars, what gives?" she asks.

"I'm to stay with him at his house for three months. Looks like he's bought me a closet full of the most beautiful clothes and shoes too, but there's a catch ..."

I wait for a response but there is none. Melly stays eerily silent.

"In return I have to be his ... companion. For the next three months I must live with him and provide him with sexual favors." I close my eyes with embarrassment as I say these things. It makes me feel dirty. I can't even begin to imagine what Melly must think of this sordid arrangement.

"That's it?" she asks, her voice astonished.

"What do you mean, that's it? Did you not hear what I said? I'm here to be his fuck buddy, Melly," I spit bitterly.

"Hold your horses, girl. Did *you* not hear what you said? A gorgeous and extremely wealthy man searched the globe for you. He's keeping you safe in his mansion, he's bought you a closet full of, I can only imagine, designer gear to put on your back and in exchange you have to sleep with this hunk? Goodness gracious, Chelsea, I wish I could be you. If a man who looked like that wanted me to be his lover, I would bloody well jump at it. No questions asked. If I thought that's what stealing three hundred thousand dollars would get me I'd become a thief tomorrow." Melly starts giggling.

Her laughter makes me laugh too. I thought for sure that she would be cursing and swearing on my behalf, but instead she's almost congratulating me. Which is weird, and oddly comforting. I was feeling dirty and she threw open a door and let the sunlight in.

"Oh silly girl. This is what the best romance fantasies are made of," she mumbles dreamily.

In the middle of my laughter, I hear the sound of the door behind me open. "I have to call you back later, Melly," I whisper quickly, and hang up. Slowly, I turn to face the door.

Thorne is standing there, his black pupils fixed on me.

THORNE

https://www.youtube.com/watch?v=nrIPxlFzDi0
(I Can't Get No Satisfaction)

I should be working now, but I've come up here like a fucking dog in heat. Panting. My cock hanging heavy and stiff.

Chelsea's eyes are large in her white face. Our gazes align exactly. For a stinking moment it feels as if I have made a terrible mistake. My stomach clenches. I should talk to her. There are so many things I want to say, but I have no words.

Then she lifts her chin proudly and walks to the armchair. She sinks into it like a Queen. "What do you want?" she asks scornfully.

No, I didn't make a mistake.

She looks like butter wouldn't melt in her mouth. She is a manipulative, lying little bitch. I was right to bring her here.

Here, I will exorcise her from my soul. I will dress her in the finest clothes, shoes, and jewelry. Then I will use her. After I am done with her I will discard her like yesterday's newspapers.

She glares at me, and I feel the anger rise within me. She stole two years of my life from me. I need to punish her, as I did in the limousine. I think about how perfect her ass looked, and I know exactly what I want to do.

Silently, I walk over to the armchair that she is seated in, and touch her face. She stiffens at the contact but doesn't move away. I get down onto my knees so we are at eye level with each other. Neither of us has uttered a word. I look down at her pink lips. They are plump, and I can already see them wrapped around my cock. My eyes glide across her face and I look at her small, upturned nose, her sparkling blue eyes, and her fair hair.

She is more beautiful now than I remember.

I place my hand on her knee without taking my eyes off her face. I slide my hand up her skirt in a way that also lifts the skirt so that it is bunched around her waist. I look at the granny panties she is wearing. They are a far cry from the lacy thong. She must have changed into this pair when I allowed her to use the bathroom in her apartment.

I grab her panties and her small teeth sink into her bottom lip. I pull the cotton material down her thighs, and toss them to the side.

She glares at me, but she says nothing. I lean my face close to hers; I don't want to miss any change of expression on her face.

My fingers dance along the soft skin of her inner thigh. I expect some token resistance, but she gives none. Well, well. She is not going to tell me to stop, nor does she look like she plans on moving away. She wants me to think she feels nothing, but little goosebumps start appearing on her skin as my fingers move higher and higher up her thigh.

I lean her back gently and she does not resist me. Just looks at me with those enormous blue eyes. I watch the pupils widen, and her mouth part as her breath comes faster. I crave the taste of her mouth so damn much it shocks me, but this is not about my pleasure.

This is about showing my total control of her body. That I can do what I want when I want with her body … now my body.

My fingers brush against the soft triangle of fair hair. She squeezes her eyes when I touch her clitoris. It is engorged with blood. Oh yes, she can lie all she wants, but she is as aroused as I fucking am.

I smile mockingly, and let my fingers wander lower until I feel how slick she is. My thumb remains on her clit and without warning I plunge two fingers into her slit. She gasps, her eyes snapping open with shock, but the expression on her face is one of defiance. She refuses to show me that she is enjoying what I'm doing to her. Her eyes stay glued to me as she tries to control her breathing. She doesn't expect my fingers to move so deeply inside her.

I'm not gentle. Why should I? She's loving this rough and after two fucking years of her absence, I deserve this. Hell, this bitch left without saying a fucking word to anyone. All those days, weeks, maybe even months that she must have meticulously planned her departure.

I thrust my fingers in and out of her, hearing the loud sucking sounds of her wet juice on my fingers. Every few thrusts, she grunts or takes in a gasping breath, but she won't give me the satisfaction of relaxing into it. She stares rebelliously at me.

With one arm holding her steady the other hand fucks her harder and faster. The walls of her pussy begin to tighten. She is so close now. My big plan was to stop. To take her to the edge and just stop. To make her beg for my cock, but I can't stop. I don't want to stop. I want to see the look on her face when I bring her to orgasm.

Finally, a low moan escapes her lips.

My thumb rubs against her hardened clit while two fingers search for her G spot. The way she is trying to stifle her moans now tells me that I've found it.

She grabs my shoulder and squeezes. I know that she can't contain herself much longer. She clenches her jaw and looks away momentarily, only she can no longer control herself. Her eyes roll back into her skull. Her body becomes limp for a moment, but that doesn't make me stop, because I know that she's ready for something bigger.

Soon she will … come again.

Chelsea lets out a loud scream and her body buckles and then shakes uncontrollably. Her thighs crush my hand, and her toes curl. There is an earthquake going off inside her, but I don't cease the thrusting of my hard fingers, not even for a moment. She groans so much I can barely hide the excitement in my eyes.

She is mine.

Whether she wants it or not she belongs to me. In my lair. Mine to do whatever I fucking please. Beholden to me until I decide to release her.

Her body is still shaking as her moans drop to soft whimpers. Her muscles take time to relax and her breathing is heavy and ragged, but now I notice that as much as she is trying to avoid staring at me, she can't. Our eyes lock. There is a strange expression in her eyes. I extract my fingers from her sweet cunt.

I want to taste her orgasm from the tips of my fingers, but now is not the right time. I stand and remove a handkerchief from the pocket in my jacket. Calmly I wipe my fingers on it.

This is called control.

Chelsea has not moved. She is just staring at me with that odd look on her face. I can't tell if there is anger in her. Her legs are still partially spread and I can see her pussy from here. It is taking all of my self-control to not lay her down and fuck her right on the chair she is seated on.

I am fully erect, but I *choose*, I force myself not to do anything about that. Not now. Not yet. Soon. Very soon.

I open my mouth to speak, but even better than words will be silence. Deliberately, I put the handkerchief back into my jacket pocket, and I turn away. I close the closet door behind me and suck the one finger I did not wipe.

She tastes like heaven.

CHELSEA

I stand in the shower while the warm water rushes down my body. It is one of those massive square shower heads so it kind of feels like I'm standing under a waterfall. I hate to admit it, but I *love* this bathroom.

Everything about it.

I love the dark blue panels, the marble fireplace, the polished dark wood floor, the double vanity, the deep claw-foot bathtub, the pots of orchids, the gilded candelabras, and this marvelous, marvelous shower.

As the water cascades down my skin, my dazed mind goes back to Thorne. Just minutes ago, I was sitting in my closet and his fingers were deep inside me. Now it feels like a fantasy. Something I dreamed up, something unbelievable. I close my eyes and remember my crazy reaction to the way he treated me, and the explosive way I climaxed.

It's never happened before.

I just don't understand what is going on. What has he done

to me? I'm supposed to be frigid, but here I am having multiple orgasms and still fantasizing about what he did to me.

My fingertips trace down the front of my body and reach for my clit. I have never been touched like that by anyone before. No one has made me come with their fingers before or given me multiple climaxes. No matter how hard I can still remember the way his thumb felt. I remember trying to resist the pull of him, but as always that was a feat impossible for me. He did it just with his fingers and without trying at all.

My whole life I believed that I always wanted a tender lover, a man who would be considerate and kind; but Thorne is rough with me. He acts like a damn caveman. He takes what he wants, and walks away without so much as a thank you, but instead of being furious he is treating me as just a sexual object, I'm aroused by it.

I thought I wanted the next ninety days to go by as quickly as possible, but that's all changed now. It's going to be really hard to continue this façade because I can pretend to hate him as much as I want, but I can't stop my body from telling him a different story. Worse, I can't help wondering if the way he makes love is anywhere near as explosive as what he does with his hands.

My clit tingles at the thought.

It's like I've gone from frigid to sex-mad. Even now, I'm desperate to touch myself and replay that scene in my head while I do it, but I can't. There was a knock a few minutes ago. Anabel sent a reminder that supper is in half-an-hour. I turn off the shower and stand in silence in the warm mist. I open the door and cold air rushes in. A memory hits. Suddenly, I am five years old again…

Twenty Years Ago

"Wake up, Papa. Wake up. There was a storm last night. There'll be loads and loads of mushrooms in the woods."

"Awfff … it's still dark outside and it's Sunday, little button," my father groans sleepily.

I shake my father's shoulder. "But you said we could go look for mushrooms today if it rained."

"Let's go tomorrow, okay. The mushrooms are not going anywhere."

I stare at him in the gloom of my parents' bedroom. "But I have to go to school tomorrow."

"Fine. I'll pick them myself tomorrow. Now go back to bed."

"No, Papa. I want us to go look for them together," I insist.

"It'll be cold and wet now. Can we go this afternoon?" he mumbles.

"No, because the wild boars will come and eat all the best ones."

My father flings one arm over his eyes. "Who told you there are wild boars on our land?"

"Monsieur Lemarie."

"Monsieur Lemarie should mind his own business," my father mutters.

I frown. "He said they come to his land too. He's seen them. They come and eat the mushrooms before the sun rises."

My father yawns. "Wild boars have to eat too."

"Right. I'll take Momo and go on my own. I know which ones are poisonous," I say decisively. It's true. I do know which ones are safe to eat. They are the ones with the spongy undersides. You can't eat the ones that have gills under their caps. My favorite is the cépe, which is never poisonous. The ones with the pretty pink pores are bitter though.

My father's eyes pop open suddenly. There is no trace of sleep in them anymore. He looks wide awake and worried. "Don't you dare go into the woods on your own. Never. Do you understand, Chelsea Appleby?"

I nod sulkily and cross my arms. "All right, but you promised we would go today," I mutter.

He sighs deeply. "Fine, we might as well go and pick these confounded mushrooms."

I throw my hands around his warm neck and squeal with delight. He laughs and envelops me within his big, strong farmer's hands.

"Can the two of you please get out of this bed and let me sleep, please?" mama mumbles irritably from under her pillow.

Papa and I laugh softly as we slide out of the bed. While my father washes up, I run downstairs and wrap up a bit of cheese in a white muslin cloth. Momo looks longingly at the cheese, so I cut a thin slice for him. He wolfs it down real quick and looks up at me with begging eyes again, but Mama says cheese is bad for dogs.

"No more," I tell him sternly.

Then, I arrange the cheese into a wicker basket with a bottle of water and half of the apple tart Mama baked yesterday. I throw in a damp cloth with which to wipe the mushrooms when we find them, and the special knife with the curved blade that Papa uses to carefully cut off the bottom of the mushroom stems. You can't just tear mushrooms out by their roots. Monsieur Lemarie says only if you are gentle with them, will they grow back in *exactly* the same spot so you know exactly where to go to pick them next year.

Once the basket is ready I fetch two sticks from the cupboard under the stairs. The longer one is for Papa and the smaller one is for me. We use them to push aside fallen leaves, and tufts of long grass to find the mushrooms hiding underneath.

By the time Papa gets dressed and comes down the stairs, I am already in my coat and rubber boots. I am so thrilled I can barely stand still. I jump up and down like a rubber ball and Momo does the same. I don't know if Momo loves mushrooming as much as I do, but he wags his tail and dashes around me in excitement.

Papa stops on the last step and smiles at me.

"Come here," he says, and crouching down, holds his arms out.

I run into his arms, but I am in no mood for a hug. "Hurry, Papa. I don't want the wild boars to eat all the mushrooms."

Papa switches on his powerful torch and we set out into the dark. It is cold and damp. Papa is holding my hand, and I'm lovely and warm in my thick coat. My heart is almost bursting with happy thoughts.

We are like Hansel and Gretel. We might find the witch's cottage, but it won't be made with sweets and chocolates, but all the different mushrooms.

Papa says that we will go into Monsieur Lemarie's woods. He was not feeling very well yesterday. We will pick the mushrooms and surprise him with our haul. I do a little skip. I love Monsieur Lemarie's woods. It is my most favorite place in the world. It will be nice if we find a lot of mushrooms for him and for us. Mama can cook them for lunch.

We follow the cycle track by the railway and go past the grassy woodland clearing. It is only after we wade knee deep in ferns that I see the shiny new car parked by the edge of the pinewood.

"There's someone in the woods, Papa," I say, tugging my father's hand.

My father frowns and quickens his pace. We enter the woods with its smell of rotting leaves and dark earth. The sky is the color of the slate on our kitchen floor, and the tree barks are pewter. Up ahead we can see a man moving slowly with his torchlight.

"Come on," Papa says.

I feel a sudden flash of fear in my stomach. I pull back. "No, Papa."

My father pulls me along.

"Hey, this is private property," he shouts when we are closer. "You are not allowed to pick mushrooms here without permission."

After that things happen so fast, I don't actually see anything, or I just can't remember. My mind refuses to see or retain. One moment Papa is talking to the man, and the next the man has lunged forward and stabbed Papa right in the middle of his chest with his knife. I just stood there. I couldn't scream, I couldn't talk, I couldn't move. I was frozen. There were no more sounds. I don't remember anything else until the skies opened, and it began to rain. A light cold drizzle.

Then the nightmare started.

CHELSEA

Wrapping myself in a thick, white bathrobe I quickly dry my hair, then pad over to the walk-in closet. I glance at the armchair and I can almost see myself writhing under him. I exhale slowly. I have to stop this.

Thorne is waiting for me. My eyes scan the massive closet. I have no idea what would be deemed appropriate for a dinner with a man who is holding me captive and using me as his sex toy. Then a stray thought enters my head: I want to look nice for him. The thought irritates me and I scowl. Why am I thinking these things?

He can own my body, but never my mind or my heart. That he must never have. Nobody will ever have that.

I walk over to the section of the closet with dresses, and I impatiently pull out the first dress in the row. I hold it up. Cream with a high neckline it is cut to be form fitting until it tapers and gently billows out at the hips. I step into the silky dress and zip it up. Then I walk to the mirror to look at myself.

Wow! It's beautiful and suits me perfectly.

I choose a comfortable pair of cream shoes with gold heels. I open a drawer and gasp. There are all kinds of accessories. Earrings, chokers, necklaces, bracelets, watches, scarves, metal belts. When Anabel said I should find everything I need here she wasn't kidding. I choose some simple gold balls for my ears, and an antique gold watch to match. Going to the dressing table I break the cosmetics out of their packages. They are not the cheap and cheerful brands I buy, but the colors are the ones I would normally go for. My look is complete when I put my dark brown hair up into a high bun.

I give myself a once-over in the mirror, but I do not let my eyes linger. I don't want to stop and think about how much money my outfit must have cost, or the fact that Thorne bought it for me. There is a gentle knock on the door. Theresa is a tiny slip of a girl. She has large anxious eyes and actually curtseys as if I am royalty or something. When I tell her to call me Chelsea, her eyes almost bulge with surprise. I want to be friends with her. Otherwise, my stay in this vast house will be difficult.

She opens the door to the dining room, then backs away the way servants of yore used to do when leaving their master's presence. I sigh. Nope. I don't think we're going to be friends. She is determined to see me as her better.

I look around me. The dining room looks like it has held many state dinners. The table is a long mahogany Munich table with about 60 dining chairs to match. Each chair has a dark purple cushion with intricate patterns in various shades of purple. The chairs that are on both ends of the table have armrests with a carved lion lying and resting. I can see that the walls of this grand dining hall have golden wallpaper on the top half. The wallpaper is striped, with some areas as matte gold and the others have a nice bright sheen. There is crown molding and carvings of cherubs and muses along the ceiling that lead to three crystal chandeliers that hang high above the dining table. The bottom half of the wall has a similar white molding with carvings all along it.

I see that the dining chair farthest from me has table settings, and I walk over to it. Just then, Thorne's butler steps out from a doorway nearest to the chair that I am about to sit in. He pulls out the chair for me, and I sit.

"Mr. Thorne apologizes for his absence, Miss Appleby," the butler says.

"Oh? He won't be joining me?" I try to hide the disappointment in my voice.

The butler smiles. Long enough for me to notice, but no longer, then he shakes his head. "No, Miss Appleby. Mr. Thorne is busy, but the Chef, Mr. Parchment, has prepared what Master Thorne believes are some of your favorite dishes."

I am stunned. What an incredible memory the man has. I only ever remember mentioning foods that I liked in passing while we were talking about an email that required us to state our food preference for a conference we were attending, and that was more than two years ago. This must be how he beats his competitors all the time. Details and control are his business. It suddenly dawns on me; that's his thing. Control.

"Thank you so much, Mr. ...," I trail away, as I realize I never got his name when I first arrived at the house.

"Just James," he says, with a slight bow of his head.

"Thank you, James." I smile at him.

He nods politely. "May I bring you an aperitif? I believe Mr. Thorne mentioned you might enjoy a dry martini."

I exhale slowly. "That would be lovely, thank you."

He nods and disappears behind the door from whence he came. I drink my perfectly shaken drink while standing by the window and looking out into the dreamily-lit formal garden. There is a massive fruit bowl filled with all kinds of ripe fruit. I look at the nectarines and feel my mouth begin to water. I haven't eaten since I've arrived and now I'm starving.

Afterwards, he serves me my favorite dishes. The Chef is superb and he manages to make leek and potato soup and shepherd's pie not only taste better than any I have had, but also look like they should be served in a top restaurant. The chocolate brownie is warm and gooey in the center, and the ice cream is homemade, and of course, it is to die for, but the whole time the thoughts that are most prevalent in my mind are:

Where is Thorne?

And why do I care so much that he is not eating with me?

THORNE

https://www.youtube.com/watch?v=-icuakaLS-A
We've Got Tonight

I glance down at my watch. Just after midnight.

The conference call lasted longer than I anticipated. I run my hand along my jaw, feeling the rasp. My shoulders feel stiff, and I've missed dinner. My stomach growls, but I ignore it.

Right now, I'm hungry for something else. I crave her and I don't think that I can wait any longer.

Rolling my shoulders, I stand and walk to the security door. I place my finger into the scanner and allow the computer to identify my iris at the same time. When the thick metal locks click, I push the door open and go up the flagstone steps into the corridor of the main house.

My shoes echo loudly in the large, silent house. All the staff has retired for the night and there is only the occasional lamp left on. I used to enjoy my solitude. I would work through the night and sleep during the day, never seeing anyone except for James. The world outside seemed unin-habitable. Full of insignificant people with their extraordinary bursts of need. Always grasping. Always wanting more from me. God, I hated people. Sometimes I wouldn't leave the dungeon for weeks at a time. I worked like a demon. Day and night. Time ceased to matter.

That was before Chelsea turned up in my life.

She turned everything I believed about myself on its head. Suddenly, I didn't find the thought of spending time with another *human* so repulsive. As much as I hated her for robbing me of my solitude, I fucking flew towards her flame like a helpless moth. My desire for her nauseated me, and the more addicted I became the more I despised myself for wanting her. Why her? She is so undeserving. A cold, manip-ulative thief. Of all the women I've met, why the fuck did it have to be her English ass that I hungered for?

I lay my foot on the first step of the stairs. God damn her, I don't even have any control of my feet. They are taking me where every nerve cell, bone, and fiber in my body is urging me to go. I walk into my room and close the door. I lean against it. I can feel my blood roaring in my ears. My pants are tight and my cock is so hard and hot it aches. It is time for me to satisfy my hunger.

My eyes move to the door that connects our rooms.

I think of her in bed beyond that door wearing the translu-cent night clothes I paid for. I think of her breathing heavily on my neck as she clenched her teeth and fought against the inevitability of her orgasm. Watching that aroused me in ways I have long forgotten. Well, I am going to remind myself of that arousal right now. I bought the privilege of rubbing my unshaven jaw against her soft skin.

Chelsea agreed to fulfill my every need. Well, I have one that wants taking care of. I need her elegant face to contort with the lust that she cannot help as I fuck her hard. I walk to the connecting door.

For a second the old habits my parents instilled in me come to the fore and I consider knocking on the door. However, she is not a guest. This is my house. I don't have to fucking knock or invite myself into any room.

I grasp the handle and push open the door.

The television is on, but it's on mute. She must have been asleep, because she lifts her head off the pillow with a confused look on her face. In the flickering blue light from the television she blinks and appears bemused by my sudden entry into her room.

"Thorne?" she asks, her voice tentative, as if I might be a dream.

I do not reply. I walk over to her and extend my hand. She looks down at it, then searches my eyes for an explanation. I cannot offer her one. I don't understand this craving for her myself.

Staring into my eyes she takes a hold of my hand. I tug her to me with enough force that she lunges towards me, her mouth opening in a scream. I catch her with ease, and lean down so that our faces are inches apart. I watch her intently. I'm waiting to see the hate in her eyes. If she hates me I can learn to hate her too. The pace of her breathing has quickened as well.

I swore I wouldn't kiss her, but fuck …

Her lips look so soft and inviting.

I can't resist her pink mouth.

My hand barely touches the side of her face, and she leans into my touch. Then she catches herself, and looks away from me. My thumb and two of my fingers grip her jaw and I turn her averted face so that she is forced to look at me. I lean in and take her mouth.

Jesus, I can't even call it a kiss. My mouth devours hers as if I'm trying to suck her very soul out of her warm mouth. The way she opens herself and melts in my arms is indescribable. If I didn't know better I would say this is the kiss of an innocent girl, not an experienced, manipulative woman. The kiss almost bewitches me …

I push her away suddenly.

"What is it?" she whispers as she moves closer to me. Her peach nightgown shimmers in the dim light. Through the delicate lace, I can see her breasts underneath. They are exactly how I dreamed they would be. Round. Her nipples are only a few shades darker than her skin. They are hard.

"Why did you come in here if this is not what you want?" she asks. Her voice is thick with passion.

I stare at her with surprise. This is the first time she's acted as if she wants to please me. I am free to have her any way I want. She owes me.

I reach for her nightgown. My hands take on a ferocious life of their own. I rip it down the middle. She doesn't flinch, just stares at me with those enormous sparkling eyes. I look at her white body while I undo my belt. Twisting the button impatiently from its eye, I slide the zipper down and shove my pants down my hips. I am so swollen and hard it actually hurts. I need to be inside her.

I push her away and she falls backwards on the bed. She lies on her back with both of her knees up. I grab hold of one of her legs and drag her towards me. Spreading her legs, I reach for her pussy, and feel how soaked her panties are. I smile at the fact that I have turned her on. Her back arches when I tease her plump clit under the fabric.

With one easy movement, I rip that last scrap of covering. She gasps and I look down at her sweet pussy, glistening like a pink oyster in the soft light. My fingers open the swollen, wet lips and expose the pearl of her clit. It reminds me of how badly I want to taste her again. I withdraw my fingers and suck them.

I push my underpants down and my cock springs out. Her eyes widen. I know my cock is big and impressive. The thick veins bulge with hot blood, making it hard as a rock. I grip my length with one hand and begin to stroke it from the base to the tip.

Chelsea hasn't moved. She watches like a woman hypnotized. She is waiting on my instructions.

THORNE

https://www.youtube.com/watch?v=_wvHVGvyUzY
Died in your arms tonight

Watching her splayed open and waiting for my cock makes me leak pre-cum. I want to tell her to lick it off, but I know I won't last if she wraps that sexy mouth around my thickness. It's her pussy that I want to feel around my cock. There will be other times to experience what her mouth feels like.

My breathing is staggered and harsh from trying to control myself.

I have a condom in my shirt pocket. I should use it. I don't know her. Where she has been. It would be wise to use it. I should. I know I should.

I grab her slim ankles, pull her to the edge of the bed, and with the backs of her calves resting on my chest, use the tip of my bare cock to find her silky wetness. She moans.

God, I have waited for this moment forever. There's no stopping me now.

I slam myself as deep inside her as I can. Her mouth opens in a soundless cry and her body jerks at the suddenness and violence of my entry. Her pussy is so tight it is like a clenched fist around my dick. When I had fingered her earlier, I knew that her pussy would be tight, but I had no idea.

Her tightness excites me to the extent I'm in danger of coming right there. I still myself deep inside her and try to hold back while she fights to adjust to my size. I look down at her and try to remember that she is an untrustworthy thief. That reminder is enough.

I pull her legs open again so that I can see everything I'm doing to her. I can see how stretched her pussy is with my cock in it. Her fair flesh impaled on my tanned cock is a sight to behold. I could watch it all night.

Chelsea coos with each throb and thrust of my cock. I begin to move my hips back and forth sliding in and out of her.

I can see it on her face. She likes having my cock buried inside her. She closes her eyes momentarily, and she groans my name under her breath. Her beautiful nipples have hardened to pebbles, and I lean over her body and bite the pink peaks. She shudders, and pushes her breast into my mouth. Begging me to suck it.

When I do she places her hands behind my head and claws at my hair. I am still pounding into her, hearing the sounds her wet pussy makes when I move in and out of her. Her pussy feels so good; so good, that I don't want it to end. It's better, by far better, than anything I imagined.

Her pussy clenches, and every time it does, my cock throbs and I know that I won't be able to hold on much longer.

I raise myself again so that I can look at her. I put each of her legs over one shoulder and hold her steady. I can't hold it any longer. I make each stroke harder and harder. Chelsea lets out moans and unintelligent whispers. Her mouth is open and she looks like she is getting closer and closer to climax.

She covers her mouth then to stifle a scream, and it angers me. I want to see everything that I'm doing to her. I want to be able to hear every sound that she makes. I spread her legs and let them collapse around my sides so that I can lean forward. I grab her by both of her wrists and then raise them over her head. She is surprised by my actions, but she understands. Now that I am over her, my pubic region can rub against her clit while I rock my hips back and forth. I feel now that Chelsea is shaking underneath me.

"Oh, my God," Chelsea gasps. Her eyes are beginning to roll back. I'm not finished with her yet. I don't want her to come yet. I slow down my strokes. Slowly and deliberately I slide in and out of her. Her pussy is so wet I feel her juice pouring over my cock.

"Do you like the way this feels?" I growl in her ear.

"Yes," she cries.

My strokes become rougher. "Do you like how I'm fucking you?" I ask again. I look into her eyes. She is quivering and squirming underneath me. I have found her spot. There is no way for her to hold in her pleasure.

"Yesss," she wails. Her eyes are wide and she is trying to pull away from me. She can't take any more of the pleasure that I'm giving her. Her gentle quivering has become a violent shake. She is ready now.

I let go of her wrists and grab her shoulders. I raise myself and begin to pound into her as deep and as fast as I can.

Chelsea screams. She's completely under my control now. I place a hand around her neck. She takes it and squeezes. Her back arches. Just as she did when I finger-fucked her. Suddenly, her body becomes limp. She sucks in a breath, then her body undulates as wave after wave of pleasure fills her. The way her pussy tightens as she hits her climax drives me insane.

The way she forces me to squeeze her throat turns me on in a way that I cannot even begin to explain. I roar as I feel that I'm about to cum inside of her. Chelsea is clawing and grabbing at me while she continues to scream and come. It's when our eyes meet again that I realize I'm coming.

I can barely control my movements, but I am still holding onto her neck and pounding her. I feel my cum jet powerfully out of me. The wetness of her pussy takes me to another dimension.

Our orgasms finish together and I collapse on top of her. We do not speak while we try to collect ourselves and catch our breath.

The encounter is incredible, but I feel as if I have dropped off a cliff. Shocked, I slide out of her and turn away.

"Thorne," she whispers.

For a second I freeze, then I turn back to look at her. The

expression in her eyes stuns me. It is almost as if she is telling me not to go. I shake the thought away. She is an expert manipulator. I brought her here against her will. I'm not going to fall for that old trick. I will not let her sink her claws into my flesh and believe that lie simply because I want her to want me as badly as I crave her.

She has lifted herself to her elbows. Her legs are still open. My eyes flick to her pussy. My cum is dripping like cream out of her reddened, puffy flesh. Something tightens inside my gut. I bring my eyes back to her face. She is watching me with that same strange expression. The air is thick with words unsaid.

Hell, I want to take her in my arms and hold her until she falls asleep. My hands clench at my sides. I can't let her see how much power she has over me. I turn and walk out of her room. I must keep my guard up.

I must not let her get to me. At the very least, she must not see how utterly, completely, and totally obsessed I am with her.

CHELSEA

I place my fingers on my neck, close my eyes, and my mind re-enacts the memory of the way his hands felt around my neck. The way he makes me lose control. That was not sex. That was us mating. On a deep and primal level. Just thinking about it makes my clit start throbbing.

I don't know what the hell is going on with me. I have never felt like this before. I did what I would never let anyone else do. I let him enter me without a condom! I wanted him to. I wanted to feel his skin. I open my eyes and stare at the canopy above the bed. I'm really confused about my own feelings. I don't understand Thorne's intentions either.

He has barely spoken to me since he punished me in the limo. I know he deliberately avoided having dinner with me. I have only seen him when he is aroused and wants to use my body to prove his control over me, or fuck me. It is clear he despises me, but he cannot resist having sex with me. There is a part of me that says it is an arrangement set up by a cold, calculating man and the less I get involved the better, but there is another part of me that wants more. Much more.

I barely sleep the whole night. Once I even got out of bed and went to put my ear to his door. It was completely silent. I went to the bathroom to wash, then I sat by the window and watched the dawn break. It's been a long time since I stayed up to watch it.

A very, very long time.

Twenty Years Ago
https://www.youtube.com/watch?v=X55nF0OqTmA
River of Tears

I look down at my father in a daze. His face is as white as a sheet. Rain is splashing onto it. The man must have taken the knife with him, because he is clutching his wound and blood is rushing out from between his fingers.

"Go get help," my father croaks.

I hear the words, but I can't move.

"Go get help, Chelsea. Hurry."

"Papa," I scream, but no sound comes out.

"Quickly, go home and wake Mama up. Tell her what happened. Bring help," he gasps.

Still I don't move.

"Chelsea," he screams.

I blink, then I drop the basket and I run. I run as fast as my legs will carry me. Twice I slip and fall on some roots, but I don't feel any pain. I just get up and keep on running. When I get home I don't clean the mud off my shoes, or stop to kiss Momo. I just run up the stairs and burst into my parents' bedroom. My mother is still sleeping. I shake her hard. She jumps with shock.

"A man stabbed Papa," I pant breathlessly.

"What?"

"In the woods. A man stabbed Papa. Quick, we have to go to him. He needs help."

My mother brushes her hair from her face and looks at me blankly. "What are you talking about?"

"Come on, Mama. We need to go now," I urge frantically.

Mama slings a coat over her nightgown and runs out into the rain with me. A couple of times Mama has to stop to bend over, to catch her breath.

"Come on," I cry with frustration.

By the time we get to Papa he has already stopped breathing. His eyes are wide open. I notice the strangest thing, then. The rain is bouncing off his eyes. I stand there and watch Mama fall on top of Papa's still body and start to wail. For ages, I stand over my parents, helpless, guilty as hell. If only I had not dragged Papa from his bed. If only I had listened to Papa and waited until the afternoon. But I was stubborn. It's all my fault.

All my fault.

CHELSEA

I gnoring the thoughts still swimming around and around in my mind like goldfish in a bowl, I make my way down for breakfast. Of course, Thorne is not there. On the snowy-white tablecloth a vast spread has been laid out. Croissants, Danish pastries, muffins, jams, biscuits, juices, cold meats. James arrives to ask if I would like a cooked full English breakfast. I tell him I am not hungry I will just help myself to black coffee and a croissant.

"Very good," he says with a nod, as he picks up the coffee pot and fills the cup in front of me.

I smile at him. "Thank you."

"I've been instructed to inform you that Mr. Thorne is expecting you to attend a luncheon at the Ritz in London with him. The car will leave at 12.20."

My eyebrows fly upwards. This must be the big unveiling of Thorne's secret new AI that James is referring to. Why is he taking me there? A lowly thief that he does not trust. All his peers, the press, anyone of any importance in the AI and robotics world will be there. I know Elon Musk is attending and so are the big guns from Google.

James wishes me a good day and silently departs.

I stare at the mini jars of jam on the table. How curious. There is even a rose petal jam from Esfahan in Iran. I pick it up and read the label. The petals are picked at dawn so they are not faded by the sun. *He wants me to go with him.* Whatever lies behind his reason, he wants me with him. The thought of him wanting me on his arm in public thrills me, but I try to push away that rush of excitement.

I unscrew the little jar and spread the rusty-colored jam on my croissant. It is too sweet. I discard it and carrying my cup of coffee walk over the enormous bay window. In the distance, I can see a man crouched on the ground. He must be one of the gardeners. He stands and kicks at the ground, and a dog runs up to him. My stomach contracts and the coffee cup in my hand rattles.

Oh, Momo!

Twenty Years Ago

"Mama."

"What?"

"There's no food in the house, and I'm hungry."

Mama turns away from staring at the urn of Papa's ashes and seems surprised. "Oh! You're hungry?"

Ever since the funeral all Mama has done is sit in Papa's favorite chair and stare at his urn. I heard Madame Bernard say that it was a kind of quiet madness. A madness designed to keep her sane. Her mind is struggling to make the world habitable again.

Of course, I don't understand what all that means, but the word mad is very worrying. I'm even afraid to go to school. One night when she was drunk on the last of Papa's whiskey, she said "Be happy, Chelsea, he's not dead at all. I promise you, he's just playing a trick on us. I think he has another woman in a different town. But he'll come back to us."

"But, Mama, his ashes are in the urn."

"Those are not his ashes. You know how big Papa was. He could never fit into that urn."

I believe her, until Monsieur Lemarie tells me that all human beings become that small when they are cremated.

Now, Mama looks around blankly. "Well, why don't you go to Monsieur Lemarie's house? His wife always has something cooking in the oven."

"Mama, will you come with me?"

"No."

"Aren't you hungry?"

She turns away from me. "No. You better enjoy your time with them. We're going back to London next week."

"What?" I gasp.

"Yes, I can't afford to live here anymore. I've already had my eviction notice. I've got you now so the government will have to house me."

"But what about Monsieur Lemarie?"

"What about him? He's nothing to us," she shoots back.

"But what about my school?"

"Well, you'll go to school in England, won't you?"

I shift from foot to foot, thinking. Two men came and bought Papa's car last week. "How will we get there?"

"I have enough for the bus."

"Will they let Momo get on the bus?"

My mother turns to look out of the window. Winter is nearly over and the snow is melting. "No, we can't take Momo with us. They'll probably stick us in a bed and breakfast to start with and pets are not allowed. I think it will be best if we leave Momo with Monsieur Lemarie."

"No, Mama. No," I cry, my eyes filling with tears.

She glares at me suddenly, her eyes cold and hard. "Are you being stubborn again, Chelsea Appleby? Have you not learned your lesson yet? Remember what happened the last time you were stubborn? Your own father was *murdered* in the woods. The next time something will happen to me. Then what will you do? Hmmm?"

CHELSEA

I decide to take a walk. It is a cold, bright morning. The air is clean and crisp. If I am lucky, I might come upon the deer herd. I walk down the road, past the tennis courts. In the distance, near a massive spreading oak tree I see them. Some are sitting quietly and the others are standing around grazing at the frost covered grass. I step off the road and start walking steadily towards them.

Some of them turn to watch me. They flick their ears and keep their gaze on me. I can see they are curious and a little wary, but they are unafraid. Slowly I go closer. One of them starts trotting away and a few follow him. I realize that I am not going to be able to go much closer. I would have loved to have gotten really close, and maybe even touch them.

I wish I had brought some food for them.

I am so focused on the deer that a sound behind me makes me jump and whirl around in fear. Thorne is heading towards me. My heart rate doesn't slow down but picks up. Somehow out here in the open land he seems bigger and more intimidating all in black, jeans, T-shirt, and leather jacket. My whole body feels uneasy. I turn back towards the deer and wait for him to arrive next to me. I watch the deer all raise their heads and watch us.

"Want to feed the deer?" he murmurs.

I look up at him. The sunlight is in his eyes, making him squint and the grey between his stubby eyelashes appear like glossy gray glass. "Yes, I'd love to."

He pulls a brown paper bag from inside his jacket.

"What is in it?"

"Strawberries," he says shaking the bag.

"They like strawberries."

"Yup. You can't just feed them anything in winter."

"Oh."

He takes a strawberry out and immediately the most daring deer starts approaching us. He stops about twenty feet away. Thorne throws the strawberry close to him. The deer moves towards the fruit, stops, looks at us and finally lowers his head and eats the fruit. Thorne flings another fruit about five feet closer. The deer moves towards the fruit. Other deer have now come to where the first deer stood.

Thorne makes a clicking, calling sound with his tongue and throws another strawberry about eight feet away from us. "It's a buck."

"Oh, my God! He's coming," I whisper excitedly. He is already so close I can see each individual strand of the fur on his body.

"Come on, big boy," Thorne encourages.

"Is he the Alpha?"

"Not sure, but he certainly is the bravest one."

The deer comes and takes the strawberry. Next Thorne throws one about three feet away. As the deer comes closer he fishes another fruit out of his bag and holds it out.

"Want another one?"

To my delight the deer trots up to him and takes it directly from his hand.

"Good boy," Thorne says and offers another strawberry. The deer takes it immediately.

"That is amazing," I gasp at that. "Can I give him one?" I ask.

"Of course." He stretches the bag out to me.

I take a fruit and hold it out by the stem. My heart is beating fast. The deer is actually a lot bigger up close than he looks from far away. He hesitates, his nostrils sniffing the air, then he comes up and quickly takes the strawberry from me.

"Oh, Thorne, I felt his lips," I say, with an awed laugh.

"Nice," Thorne says, but he is looking at me in a strange way.

I realize that I could be showing Thorne the side of me that I don't want him or anyone else to see. I compose my face. "Can I have another one?"

He holds the bag out to me. "Take the bag, but throw some to the other boys too. Look at them. They want some, but they are just too timid."

"Okay." I throw some to them and watch them eat the fruit, but my real love is for the brave boy who dared come so close to us. I wish I could pet him, but he has a substantial rack, and I can imagine how badly I would be injured if he rammed me.

When the strawberries are all gone, the deer moves away. I stare at it longingly, but I am intensely aware of Thorne standing next to me.

"Do you want to see the lake?" he asks.

"There is a lake?"

"Uh … huh."

"If you have nothing better to do." I don't know why I said that. I'm not usually such a sap.

"I have nothing better to do," he says quietly. "Come on."

He sets up a brisk pace and we walk in silence. Just over the rise we come upon the lake, surrounded by trees. It is wonderfully peaceful. Sunlight bounces off the water, and swans and ducks swim serenely on the sparkling surface. It is very, very beautiful. How lucky he is? He owns all this.

"You're a very lucky man, Throne."

He frowns. "I never thought about it, but I suppose I am."

"You never thought about it?"

"No. I spend so many hours working I never have time to enjoy any of this."

"Really? Seems such a shame. To have all this and never appreciate it."

He glances at me. "You are right. I need to hit my off button more often."

"Where is it? I'll do it for you?" I offer.

He laughs.

I stare up at him. When he laughs like this he is indescribably splendid. I watch him closely. I want to remember this moment. One day he will be gone, but I will have this enchanted moment by the lake forever.

"What is it?" he asks, suddenly frowning.

"Nothing," I say quickly.

"Hmmm."

"There is a boat. Do you row?"

"Nah. I've never been on the lake."

"I've always wanted to be on a rowing boat. Can we have a go?"

He stares at me. "You really want to?"

"Yes, of course."

"It won't be too cold for you?"

"No. I think I am secretly an Inuit. I never feel the cold."

He helps me into the boat. To be honest it is quite small and rickety and a little voice at the back of my mind does worry that we might end up in the freezing water, but I know I can never say no to this experience. One day when I'm lying on my death bed I will remember, I rowed on a lake on a bright cold morning with an elusive billionaire called Thorne Blackmore.

Thorne's powerful arms row us to the middle of the lake. I look around me. It is exactly what I thought it would be. Magical. I gaze into his face. "Thank you for this," I whisper.

"No, thank you, Chelsea. My life is staring at computer screens. If you had not brought me here, I would never have known how beautiful the lake is."

Something inside me relaxes. For these few moments, he is not Throne Blackmore the elusive and cold billionaire, he is a man rowing a woman on a lake. "It is beautiful, isn't it?"

"You have no idea how beautiful," he says, but he is not looking at the lake. He is looking directly into my eyes.

CHELSEA

A luncheon at the Ritz will require a beautiful and bright cocktail dress. I stand in front of the closet and let my eyes move along the color coordinated rack of clothes.

Then I see it. A fitted hot pink dress with a low neckline and a cute peplum. It could work, but it is brighter than I was thinking of. For a winter occasion … I hesitate, unsure if it's something I can pull off, but the dress is so beautiful I can't bring myself to put it back on the rack.

What the hell. I'll just try it on and see what it looks like.

I slip it on and to my surprise it looks really, really good on me. I don't think I have ever worn something so effortlessly classy. It must cost the very earth. I turn around and twist back to look at the dress from the back in the mirror. The dress hugs me in all of the right places and cleverly accentuates my small bum so it looks quite substantial. Whoever Thorne hired to stock this wardrobe for me really knows their stuff.

Helpfully, that person also put a pair of black Manolo Blahniks directly underneath. The back of the shoe is adorned with a tiny black ruffle along the front that goes perfectly with the peplum on the dress.

I take the time to make my eyes smoky. It highlights the blue of my eyes. I find a lipstick to almost exactly match my dress. That goes on next. An updo would be too formal for a luncheon, so I clip my hair back with black velvet clips.

After I give myself a quick once-over and decide that I feel confident with the end result, I spray some perfume from a selection of bottles on the dressing table. I'm not sure who I'm trying to impress, but I must kill the excitement that is uncoiling at the pit of my stomach when I think of how Thorne will react to my appearance.

Feeling confident I shrug into a black velvet coat and leave the room. I meet Anabel coming from the other end.

"Oh my, oh my, lass. You'll knock the spots off all the other women," she says with a cheeky grin.

I smile back shyly. "You don't think it's too bright?"

"Child. You're a sight for sore eyes." She leans forward. "And Mr. Thorne's eyes are very sore these days. He works too hard." She tuts. "Too many hours that man puts into his work."

I blush.

"Well, I won't hold you back. I just came by to see if everything was to your satisfaction. And if you need anything else."

"Yes, everything is just great. Thank you."

She turns to go, then whirls back. "Oh, and you don't need to make your own bed. Theresa will come around to do it while you are at breakfast and if you decide to have breakfast in bed, she will do it when you leave."

"I don't mind."

"I know, child, but you wouldn't want to put Theresa out of a job now, would you?" she says with a wink.

I smile and shake my head. She goes the way she came and I descend the stairs. Halfway down I am suddenly incredibly nervous. I pause and give myself a small pep talk. *You're simply going to be Thorne's arm candy for the day. Don't allow yourself to fall into the trap of thinking that you are anything more than just a trophy that he is using for his pleasure.*

As I resume my journey down, Thorne steps into the hallway and looks up at me. My breath hitches. He is in an immaculate dove-gray suit, white shirt, and charcoal tie. It's not something I expected. I've never seen him in anything but black. Black suits, black T-shirts, black jeans. His hair is pulled back and out of his face, and he is freshly shaved.

He looks incredible.

His lips part when he sees me, but instead of his usual scowl or cold nod of acknowledgement, he becomes completely still. He stares at me almost in disbelief, or shock. It's like he is seeing me for the first time. Then he blinks, and the stunned look is gone from his face.

He walks towards me and, as he did the night before, he extends his hand out to me. I don't hesitate this time. When I place my hand in his, he rubs the back of my hand with his thumb and brings it to his lips. My whole body tingles with electricity.

"Will I do?" I breathe.

"You'll do, Chelsea Appleby," he murmurs against my skin.

My tense body relaxes, melts like chocolate in the summer. I stare up into the beautiful icicles in his gray eyes. How long I was lost in their desolate beauty I don't know. It could have been a few seconds, a few days, or even years, but I know I wanted to stay there forever.

There is a cough to the left of us, and I jump and whirl my head towards the sound. For a moment there, we were the only people in the universe. No one else existed.

"Ryland is bringing the limousine around," James says.

We walk together to the front door as the car rounds the fountain and pulls up by the steps.

James moves forward to open and hold the door for us.

CHELSEA

"So this is the big unveiling?" I ask into the strange silence between us.

He nods. "Yes."

"Are you nervous?"

He looks at me curiously. "Why would I be nervous?"

I shrug. "I don't know. The unveiling is a very big thing, isn't it? The whole world is waiting to see what you come up with. All the knives are out. Everyone is waiting to criticize."

"Shall I tell you a secret?"

My eyes widen. "Okay."

He leans forward, his eyes strange and unknowable. I think this is the moment I finally admit to myself: I'm in love with this man. I have been for years. I just refused to acknowledge it. Now, I can no longer run away from the knowledge.

"All is just a party trick, a sleight of hand. Like someone who pulls out a coin from behind your ear. She is already surpassed," he says, a mocking tilt to his voice, his breath warm against my neck.

"Allí?" I whisper.

He moves back to look into my face. "Is the AI robot that will be unveiled today."

I try to assimilate what he is saying. "What do you mean?"

"What they will be celebrating today is already old news. I have built an AI that if unleashed will make the world as we know it unrecognizable."

I stare at him. I don't know much about AIs, but I am vaguely afraid of them. I have been ever since I read an article from Steven Hawkins warning us of the dangers of AI. "What kind of changes are we talking about?"

He laughs. "You are a thief and a liar, what makes you think I would tell you?"

That hurt is palpable. I feel in my chest a sharp stab. I turn away from him blindly.

"Chelsea?" he calls, his voice odd, but I don't turn around. I can't let him see how much he has hurt me.

"Keep your secrets, Thorne. I don't want to know. I was just making polite conversation."

The rest of the journey is managed in tight, tense silence. I can hear him breathe, smell his cologne, see the perfect crease of his trousers, but we might as well have been on different planets. My heart feels numb.

I n spite of the fact the exact location was only revealed to people on an individual basis based on how long the journey will take them to arrive here, someone has managed to alert the paparazzi. They line the perimeter of the hotel and across the street with the long-lens cameras. They are all expecting to see Thorne, but the driver drops us off at the back where the organizers are waiting with a whole load of security men.

I'm actually surprised at how much security there is.

It's quite unnerving because everybody stares at me. I know they are surprised to see Thorne, a fiercely private and inscrutable man, bring a woman with him. They have never seen him with one before. He leads me inside to meet some of the people. I start to recognize some of the world's most famous billionaires. Hell, you couldn't swing a cat without hitting a famous person.

I try to be as gracious as I can when Thorne introduces me to the bright sparks of his industry, but it is impossible for me to remember their names or faces. There are so many of them and they all wear the same awed expression when they are talking to Thorne.

I see a different side of him. He is the star of this show. Everybody wants a piece of him. I take a step back and study his confident, relaxed demeanor. I know it is a mask, so very different from the dark, brooding man I know. I wonder about his AI. All these people think what they are seeing is the latest and most advanced technology, but Thorne has kept the best for himself.

A beautiful blonde woman walks up to us. Even before she

reaches us, my hackles rise and my body is on alert. She is taller than me, and her glittering green eyes flash between me and Thorne. A corner of her mouth twists upwards, but it's not a friendly smile.

"Chelsea Appleby meet Andrea Bloom," Thorne introduces.

I smile and hold out my hand. She offers me a limp hand and flashes another fake smile.

"Well, well, Chelsea Appleby. You've made quite a catch there," she drawls looking down at me.

If I were in a different surrounding I would know exactly how to answer her, but this is Thorne's big moment and I'm not going to be the one who makes a scene. I force a polite smile. "How is it that you two know each other?"

"We used to date a lifetime ago, but Thorne turned out to be so extremely driven and ruthless there was no place for a woman in his life." She looks up at Thorne and winks at him. "Looks like that is no longer true."

I can see right through her. She is making a play for him. My stomach burns as if I have drunk battery acid. The effortless way he hurt me in the car replays in my mind and I try to tell myself he doesn't belong to me, but nothing can ease the fire in the pit of my belly. She wants him. Oh, God, maybe he wants her too. The thought is too painful to bear.

"Anyway, that's all in the past," she says with a little laugh, and her eyes turn back to me. She glances at my dress and takes a sip of her champagne. "Is that a Chiara Boni?"

I touch the dress self-consciously. "Yes, I think so."

Her eyebrows lift mockingly. "You're not sure? How utterly charming."

I feel myself flush. "Ooo …" she coos. "How sweet. A girl who blushes." She looks up and sideways at Thorne, a practiced, seductive gesture. "Where on earth did you find this creature? She's absolutely entertaining."

I dare not look at Thorne. If I look at him and catch him returning her desire, I will be physically sick, or I will scratch her eyes out. The bitch looks at me again. "Don't take anything I say to heart. I'm just a terrible tease. I only do it to the people I like. I wouldn't dare wear that color, but it's a delightful dress, and it certainly suits you."

God, she is so phony, I can't stand it. I thank her for her empty compliment, then immediately excuse myself to search for the restroom. This is a mostly-men affair and there is no one inside, thank God. Stepping inside, I move to the mirror.

I just need a few moments to myself to clear my head.

CHELSEA

Standing over the sink, I rest my hands on it. I close my eyes and take in a few deep breaths. Suddenly the door opens, and Andrea is standing there with a smirk on her face. Our eyes meet in the mirror.

"Hello again," she says, and this time there is no sweet smile. The gloves are off. No one is around and she doesn't have to pretend.

"What can I do for you?" I do not try to hide my distant tone.

"Just came to tell you not to get too comfortable as Thorne's latest squeeze," she says.

"Excuse me?"

"Thorne becomes infatuated with a bright young thing every once in a while. It's his way to relieve the tension of being cooped up for days on end by himself talking to those robots."

I frown.

"Oh, you poor thing. Did you not realize that the man has no time for a real relationship? He just needs a body, any body, to satisfy his impressive sexual appetite," she says as she walks over to me. Instead of looking directly at me, she stares condescendingly at my reflection in the mirror.

I don't look away. I don't want to show any kind of weakness around her. "That doesn't bother me," I lie.

She laughs. "It's just a bit of friendly advice, woman to woman, but if you're into being used, go for it. Enjoy it while it lasts, girlie. Trust me, when Thorne finds someone else, the fancy dinners, the expensive dresses, the Louboutins, the parties, and all of the romance … well, you can kiss them all goodbye, and go right back to wherever it is you came from."

She smiles again, but it isn't a fake smile she presented before. It is a triumphant smirk. I want to wipe the smile off her face with a slap, but a lump in my throat catches me off guard. She flounces out of the Ladies. I tell myself she knows nothing about me. Nothing.

I look in the mirror and all I see are my lips. Hot pink.

Twenty years ago

England is so cold and gray. Mama and I sit on plastic chairs in a waiting room of the Social Services office. Everybody here is pale and seems unhappy. We are sitting near an old man who smells of wee. He smiles at me and I try to smile back, but I can't because I am so unhappy and frightened of what will happen next. Already I have lost Papa, Momo, and Monsieur Lemarie. All my friends are gone too. All I have left is Mama, but she won't even look at me. She stares straight ahead.

Now she turns to me. "When they call us in I want you to cry and look pitiful."

"What if I can't?" I whisper back.

Something cold and hateful flashes in her eyes. "Why don't you think of Papa or Momo?"

Surprised by Mama's tone I say nothing else and stare ahead of me. When Mama's name is called, we go into a cubicle and sit in front of a woman with bored eyes and untidy hair. Her name is Mrs. Stevens. Mama carefully puts the urn with Papa's ashes on the table. Mrs. Stevens raises her eyebrows in a kind of disbelieving way.

As soon as Mama starts telling our story she starts sobbing, but Mrs. Stevens seems completely unmoved. She just dumps a box of tissues next to the urn for Mama to use. Sometimes, she makes notes on a form she pulled out of her drawer when we first walked in.

Mama lays her hand on my head. "This poor child has hardly eaten for days. She blames herself for her father's death. She suffers from terrible nightmares. I am so afraid for her. She may be damaged forever."

I see Mrs. Stevens's eyes flick down towards me so I quickly think of Papa and Momo and my eyes fill with hot tears that start rolling down my face. Although Mrs. Stevens was unmoved by Mama's tears, she frowns when I start crying. I look at Mama and she smiles approvingly at me. So I cry even more.

"It's okay, sweetheart. It's okay. You'll be fine. Do you want a biscuit?" she coos in a high voice.

I know she is being kind, but it shocks me that she thinks she can replace Papa and Momo with a biscuit. I'm not hungry, but I nod, because I can see that it is what Mama wants me to do. Mrs. Stevens opens a bottom drawer and takes out a packet of tea biscuits and holds it out to me. I wipe my tears and take a biscuit.

Mama and me spend that night in a bed and breakfast. There are many families like us living there. We see them sitting around talking in the lobby downstairs as we check in. I spy two girls who are my age. One of them waves to me and I wave back shyly.

I make friends with them the next morning at breakfast. Their names are Heather and Sylvia. Heather has a rabbit in her room.

"I thought animals are not allowed," I whisper.

"That's right, but I smuggled Harry in. Loads of us do it. Didn't you bring yours, then?" she whispered back.

"Mama didn't know we could," I say sadly.

"Well, get someone to send him to you," Sylvia suggests.

I decide to write to Monsieur Lemarie and ask him to please bring Momo to us, but when I give Mama my letter she tears it into pieces.

"What a selfish little brat you have become. Is this really where you want Momo to live? In this dump? In France he can run in the fields and go where he wants. Here he will be trapped in this small, stinking room day and night. Sometimes, Chelsea …"

Social Services finally finds a small apartment in the beginning of summer for us. Mama is very happy. On the first night we move in she pulls out her little black dress with the lace sleeves that Papa bought for her, shaves her legs and pulls on her lovely black stockings. Then she paints her mouth with her hot pink lipstick and goes out for a drink with a man she met at the bed and breakfast.

When she came home in the early morning hours, the hot pink lipstick was gone from her lips.

CHELSEA

Someone comes into the restroom. She smiles at me. I smile back, then I turn away from the mirror, open the bathroom door and let myself out. My eyes immediately search for Thorne. I find him near the stage. He is speaking to Andrea Bloom. Unseen by them, I stare at the picture they make. She is laughing at something he says and gently touches his sleeve. The gesture is possessive. Every person who looks at them will think they are together.

I feel sick.

I want to run up to her and knock her head off. I need to forget this feeling. I want to forget ever meeting Andrea Bloom.

"Chelsea? Chelsea Appleby?"

I turn at the sound of my name. I haven't seen the man smiling at me in years, but of course, I remember him. He is someone who used to supply the robotics side of Thorne's business. He's a handsome older gentleman with silver hair and flinty blue eyes.

"Monsieur Blanchett," I say with a smile. It's nice to see a familiar face. He has always been very kind to me, so I'm glad to see him. Being French he air-kisses my cheeks three times.

"It's been so long. What brings you back to these parts?" he asks in French.

I glance over at Thorne, who is still talking to Andrea. I feel the pain in my belly, but I turn my full attention to Monsieur Blanchett.

"Thorne and I recently reconnected. I just got into the country yesterday," I reply in French.

"Oh!" He can't help the speculative look that comes into his eyes. "That's nice. How long will you be staying in England?"

"Three months. I'll be around for the next three months." If Thorne is finished with me by the beginning of next month then that means I will be free of my debt to him. I will be able to return to New York and go back to my old life.

"Ah."

"So you still do business with Thorne?" I ask, trying my best to concentrate on his answer and not turn around to stare at Thorne and Andrea. From the corners of my eyes I can still see the flash of her blonde head, but I avoid looking in their direction.

"But of course. He is the most important person in AI development."

I nod.

"Do you still work for Thorne?" he asks, turning to look around the room. He is looking over my shoulder and even getting onto the balls of his feet in order for him to be able to scope the room. "Where is Thorne anyway?" he asks.

I turn to see if Thorne is still with Andrea, but both have gone. Jealousy and anger swell within me.

"No, I'm not working for Thorne anymore." My answer is honest.

Monsieur Blanchett stops looking around and smiles at me. "Well, it would be lovely to catch up. May I invite both Thorne and you to have lunch with me next week?"

'I'm sorry. I don't know what Thorne's schedule is like."

"Well, you are welcome to come on your own. You can tell me … how do you say it … what the devil … you have been up to since you ran away without telling a soul."

I blush, then laugh.

Monsieur Blanchett chuckles. "And I can bore you by talking shop." I like him. I've always liked him. He reminds me of Monsieur Lemarie. Like me, he too has an appreciation for numbers.

"Lunch sounds lovely. I'd love to come," I tell him.

"Fabulous. I will get my secretary to call you and set something up."

"Excuse me …" snaps Thorne.

I am startled because I did not notice Thorne walking up to us. Monsieur Blanchett smiles.

"There you are, Thorne. This beautiful woman of yours and I were just—" Mr. Blanchett begins, but Thorne cuts him off.

"I don't have time for niceties, Blanchett. We're leaving, Chelsea," Thorne bites out rudely, while glaring at me.

Monsieur Blanchett looks shocked.

"But what about the unveiling—," I blurt out, confused and embarrassed.

"Can be accomplished without me. Come," he almost snarls.

My head jerks back and my whole face burns. He is treating me as if I am a naughty child in a public place. I feel bad for Monsieur Blanchett too. He did nothing wrong.

I open my mouth to protest, but the way Thorne's nostrils flare and his eyes narrow tells me that I'm better off keeping my mouth shut. As Thorne lays claim to his ownership of my body by slipping his hand around my waist, I give Monsieur Blanchett an apologetic look. Without a word, Thorne leads me towards the back entrance.

I'm beyond furious. He has made a complete fool of me, but I don't say anything. Let him have his control. Better this than prison.

THORNE

I am so fucking furious I don't — actually fuck don't, can't — say a word to Chelsea on the drive home. Jesus, I can't even look at her. My blood is boiling in my veins and I want to punch something. Hard.

"Come to my study," I order when we arrive at the house. She looked confused and hurt when I didn't want to tell her about my AI and I actually felt bad, but what an idiot I was. I turn my back on her for one second and she's accepting lunch dates with another man. Fuck her and that old fool. He thinks he can handle her. This bitch will have him wrapped around her little finger and licking her boots before long.

I walk ahead of her, deliberately keeping my stride long. Behind me, I hear the sound of her shoes as she quickens her pace to keep up with me. I open the door and hold it for her. She walks through, her eyes staring straight ahead, and turns around to face me defiantly.

I count to ten to calm my nerves. She's so unbelievably untrustworthy. What the fuck am I even doing with her? I should kick her out of my house. She's turning my life upside down. The longer I keep her here, the more enslaved I become to her body.

I thought overindulgence would cure me. If I overdose on her body, twice, three, four times a night, I will tire of her smell, her taste, her feel, but she is like a disease inside me. Spreading. There is an old Indian saying I should have taken heed: indulging in desire is like pouring clarified butter onto fire. It doesn't quench the flames, it fans it.

I should tell her to go.

"You're mine, Chelsea," are the words that come out of my mouth. The rest comes out as a growl throbbing with aggression and jealous anger. "For the next three months I own you. You are fully paid for, which means you cannot flirt with another man. You cannot accept lunch dates. You cannot touch another man. And no man can touch you. Do you understand me?"

"It didn't mean anything. He's a nice guy," she whispers.

"I don't give a fuck whether it means anything or not. You do not talk, hell, you do not even look at another man for the next three months. Do you understand me?"

She stares at me in shock. She opens her mouth to say something, then she drops her head and nods. I am not satisfied with that response.

I take a step forward and she steps back nervously. I make another move towards her, and she counters it with a move in the opposite direction. We play this game until her butt bumps into my heavy mahogany desk.

With a slow, cold smile, I take the final step in her direction.

She stares up at me, a strange expression of desire and fear frozen on her face.

My large hands land on her waist.

She draws a sharp breath, but makes no protest. I let my hands run down the shapely curve of her hips. Then I pull the skirt of her dress up until it is bunched around her hips. Wrapping my hands around her I pick her up and sit her on the desk. Roughly I spread her legs. She searches my eyes. She knows what's going to happen to her next, but she doesn't stop me. She just licks her lips and pretends she doesn't want it.

My arms go under her thighs to bring her closer to the edge of the desk. How sweet, a little pink G-string is all there is between me and her pretty pussy. I tear off the scrap of lace and fling it behind me. She groans and I sense the heat and tension in the air.

"You're wet, my darling," I mock.

She swallows hard, but doesn't say anything while I look at her open pussy. My cock is throbbing for her. I want to be inside her right now, but she has to be reminded of who she belongs to. She is going to enjoy everything that I do to her on this desk or I'll be damned.

I widen her legs further and she leans back on the palms of her hands.

I lower myself onto my knees and the scent of her makes my head spin. Fuck her, and her magic spell. I bury my face between her legs. In reflex, her hand moves to grab the back of my head and push me closer to her.

I smile as I lick and suck at her wet folds. Her pussy tastes so sweet to me, and I lick the opening all the way up to her plump nub. Chelsea moans and claws the back of my head. She is completely enjoying herself and that makes me enjoy her even more.

Her legs are over my shoulders now, she is using them to steady herself as the feeling inside of her becomes more intense. She asks me what I'm doing to her, but I don't answer. She doesn't seem to notice since her moans have become much louder.

I suck on her clit while using my tongue to lick the very tip. The different sensations cause her to shake and her legs begin to clench my head. She is on the edge of climaxing. What I'm doing feels so good to her that her body begins to quiver uncontrollably. Clenching her teeth, she grips my head and pulls me in as if she wants to be swallowed by me.

A long high pitched moan escapes her lips.

I love the animalistic cries she is making, almost as much as I love the sound her pussy makes against my tongue. It is the delicious sound of wetness and pleasure. She is so wet for me. Eating her out makes me even more hungry for her. After this I will take her, but I need her to cum on my tongue first. I need to drink her into my system.

She is shaking so much now I hold her steady on the desk as I continue to suck and lick her. I flick my tongue against her clit, then thrust it hard inside of her, and that is when she falls backwards.

I hear her saying "Oh my God" over and over.

Chelsea's legs tighten like a noose around me, then suddenly release as she lets out a final and very long scream of ecstasy. It just goes on and on.

It doesn't stop me.

I lick the juice that gushes out of her while I wait for her scream to fade into gentle purrs. She has reached her climax and she's satisfied. I'm not. The memory of her flirting with Blanchett is still fresh in my mind. I still have more I want to do to her. I give her a moment and then scoop her limp body up into my arms.

I step on her panties on the way out of my study.

CHELSEA

https://www.youtube.com/watch?v=-rey3m8SWQI&index=9&list=RDMM9JntzkszLX8

Be The One

The orgasm I just experienced was so incredibly intense my body feels heavy and satiated, as if I've been drugged. I press up against Thorne's hardness, and clutch at his broad shoulders with my fingertips. My eyelids flutter downwards with a strange exhaustion. Thorne is carrying me up the stairs as if I weigh no more than a child.

I force my eyes open and almost in a daze watch the harsh line of his clenched jaw. The way this man touches me, and licks me, and fucks me is completely different from anything I have ever felt or experienced with anyone else.

The orgasms he brings me actually make me forget who I am. During them I exist only as a point of pleasure in the universe. I won't admit I'm addicted to the way he makes me feel, but that's just me lying to myself.

He opens a door and I recognize the faint scent of the perfume I used. We're in my bedroom. Thorne kicks the door closed and carries me to the bed. Instead of putting me down, he kisses me.

My mouth opens to receive his tongue. I suck it mindlessly, sighing restlessly when he withdraws it.

"Bend over the bed, Chelsea," he growls into my ear.

He sets me on my feet by the bed and looks at me. I'm glad the lights are off or he might be able to see the greedy expression on my face. Though I'm utterly spent, my insides suddenly become intensely alive and vibrant. I can feel my body humming.

I can't wait to feel him again.

Thorne rolls my dress up and slaps my ass. I gasp at the unexpected sting. I hear the sound of a zip being opened as he removes his pants and begins to rub up against me. God, he is so hard it makes me wet all over again. He moves his thick shaft towards my center. I find myself tense and desperately waiting for that first feeling, the first stroke of sheer bliss when he plunges inside me.

Soon, I feel the silky head as it forces its way inside me.

His entry is slow, as if he's savoring the feeling of my tightness around him. I clutch the bedspread, getting used to his size and the total power he has over me. He moves his body over mine so that he is lying across my back. One of his arms wraps around my waist while the other searches for my clit in the dull afternoon sun. When he finds it, he moves his hand in slow circular motions. His deep strokes and the way he caresses my clit are enough to have me nearly at the edge of another climax.

I didn't think it was possible for sex to ever feel this good.

Every part of my body is tingling with the sensations his body is causing. I almost want to cry, but I barely make a sound. I am too focused on the incredible sensation of his hand massaging my clit and the slow and deep strokes of his cock moving inside of me.

The pleasure is too much for me and a whimper escapes my lips.

He groans in my ear and quickens his thrusts. Each stroke becomes deeper. I love the slight pain I feel from how deep he is going. I want it to hurt. I wanted this feeling to last all afternoon, all evening, all night. I don't want it to stop. Ever.

Thorne bites down on my shoulder and begins to suck. The way any part of his body touching me sets me on fire is astonishing. My hand reaches for the arm that he has wrapped around my waist.

I grip it tightly as the sounds of our mating fill the room. It's impossible to pretend it doesn't feel as amazing as it does. No amount of holding back will convince Thorne, Besides, I don't want to deny this amazing feeling. It was hard enough even getting me off once, let alone multiple orgasms.

I moan his name. It sounds good in my mouth and it makes him rub my pussy faster. I want to see his face, the expression in his eyes. He groans, and the sounds of his pleasure turn me on even more, though I didn't think that such a thing was even possible.

His pace quickens and he thrusts in and out of my pussy with intense speed and power. My body starts to shake. It won't be long now before I reach another peak. I almost don't want to climax. I want this to last longer.

My arms buckle and my head and upper body fall to the bed now. I bite down on the bedsheets to try to control the sounds that I'm making even though I know that no one can hear us. Thorne raises himself off me and, holding my waist with both of his hands, pounds into my pussy. He is moving so fast and so deep now that my eyes begin to roll back. My body shivers under him as I wait for the earth-shattering orgasm to hit.

"Whose pussy is this?" he grunts through gritted teeth. I can't reply. The sound of his voice coupled with his heavy breathing is about to send me over the edge.

"I said whose pussy is this?" he asks more forcefully, as he slams even deeper into me.

"Yours!" I scream, and that is when I feel it. The delicious sensation that erupts from my very core. Thorne pulls out then and puts his tongue on my pussy. He tastes me as my body spasms with indescribable pleasure, before shockingly, opening his mouth wide and sucking, almost swallowing, my entire pussy. It is the most amazingly possessive thing anyone has ever done to me.

I suck in a long, shuddering breath as Thorne holds me firm in his mouth until my orgasm dies away. Then before I can even recover properly, he is back inside me, pumping relentlessly. He makes me come again before he allows himself to release his hot seed deep inside me.

I am so completely exhausted, I can't even move my body, I

lay unmoving as Thorne pulls out and collapses onto the bed next to me. I look into his eyes. In the slanting light his eyes shine like gray jewels between his half-hooded lids. I stare into them. I love him. I love him so much it tears me up inside because I know it's like loving a snake. It will never love you back. It doesn't know how to. He is the perfect man to develop an unfeeling robot.

He lifts his arm and starts to unzip my dress.

"I can't take anymore," I whisper.

"I know. I just want to see you naked." His voice is mellow. I haven't heard it like that before.

I allow him to undress me. He takes my bra off and cannot help himself. He bends his head and sucks my nipples. One after the other. I gasp at the sensation.

"I want more, but you're tired and I haven't slept in twenty hours," he mutters. Picking up my nude body, he puts me under the covers. I watch Thorne remove his clothes and, to my great surprise, join me beneath the sheet.

"Go to sleep, Chelsea," he says, wrapping a heavy arm around me.

I close my eyes obediently. It doesn't take long before sleep comes to collect me.

THORNE

https://www.youtube.com/watch?v=qEd6QUbK2Mw
(Making Love Out Of Nothing At All)

I'm dragged out of some deep dream, my eyes snapping open suddenly. My brain is only half-present, but it instantly notes that I'm not in my own room even though it is dark. The sound that woke me up comes again. Someone's voice. Chelsea's. I raise my head and turn to peer at her. In the dark her skin glows like porcelain.

"What is it?" I ask.

She doesn't respond to me. She shifts and rolls over to face me.

"No," she mutters, "don't touch me."

I stare at her. Her eyes are closed. She is talking in her sleep. I know I should wake her up, but I cannot resist the opportunity of seeing behind the mask. Listening to her most private thoughts. Those only expressed in her dreams.

She starts writhing violently, as if trying to escape from an assailant in her dream realm. Holy hell, she's not dreaming. She is having a nightmare.

I can't watch any longer. Gently, I shake her shoulder and Chelsea jerks awake and instinctively scoots away from me. Her eyes are wide with fear and she is breathing hard.

"Hey, it's only me," I say, and pull her unresisting body towards me. Her heart is pounding so hard that I can feel it. She is so upset she forgets her normal reserve. Wrapping her arms around me she begins to cry softly.

"Shhh … I'm right here. Everything is all right," I croon, running my hand up and down her bare back. Reassurance is all that I can offer her without knowing what it is that has her so afraid.

"Tell me what's wrong?" I whisper into her silky hair, when the sobbing stops.

Just as suddenly as she came to me, she suddenly pulls away. She wipes her tears and lies back on the pillows, staring at the opposite wall. "It was nothing. Just a bad dream," she mumbles.

This is a side of her that I have never seen before. Chelsea has always been pragmatic, practical, intelligent, hidden, and most of all distant. To see her now so shaken up makes me feel as if I've never known her.

"What did you dream about?" I ask.

She doesn't look me in the eye. "It's nothing."

The pinched expression on her face is the best evidence for why that simply isn't true. "If there is anything I can do to help you …"

She shakes her head. I am about to speak up again, when she turns around and bites down on my bottom lip, then starts kissing me ferociously. Almost as if she wants to consume me. I know what that feels like. I know she is doing that because she doesn't want me prying into her dream, but it's impossible to resist her now. I *want* to be consumed by her.

She maneuvers her body quickly, her breasts bouncing in the gloom, and climbs on top of me. She hovers over me like an avenging angel, and blood rushes to my cock, electrifying me. I bend upwards to reach her.

I close my eyes as she trails delicate kisses down my neck. My body tenses as she sinks her teeth into my neck. Chelsea taking charge and trying to overpower me is a new and sexy feeling. I feel her lay her tongue on my skin to taste my heartbeat in the blood that flows under my skin. From my neck down to my bare chest she goes.

Her tongue makes circles around my nipple, then she sucks on it.

She pushes me down so that I am lying back on the pillows. Then she straddles my thighs. She is so wet, she leaves a wet patch on my skin. She wraps her hand around my shaft, then lifts her body over it. I don't thrust upwards. I let her take charge. She impales herself on my cock beautifully, her mouth opening in a soundless cry of pleasure.

With my cock buried deep inside her Chelsea starts playing with her breasts, squeezing and rubbing them. Her silhouette is beautiful, unforgettable. Her face is contorted. She tilts her body and rocks her hips back and forth so my cock is moving back and forth inside of her pussy.

Then Chelsea leans forward and allows her hips to move in a circular motion. I can feel her clit, rubbing, rubbing, rubbing. Her movements are rough and fast.

"Yesssss," she hisses, lost in the sensations her body is feeling.

Though I enjoy it, I can sense that she is not completely here with me. She isn't taking her time. She wants to come and she wants to come now.

I sit up and hold her, my hands gripping her by her waist so that her movements remain steady and fluid. Then I thrust my hips to match her rhythm. Moving with her is my way of letting her know I am here with her; that whatever it is that scared the hell out of her in her nightmare doesn't mean shit to me.

Our agreement included me protecting her as if she is part of me.

I stare into her face, watching the emotions of pleasure and lust and need and greed. I catch her hips and pull them up and down so she is no longer gyrating into me. Now she is bouncing on my dick, but at her own pace and to her own rhythm. She is going at me hard. My grip on her tightens. My mouth opens in a groan.

"Chelsea, you're gonna make me cum."

"Cum for me," she orders.

I stare into her beautiful eyes. Fuck, she has never been more beautiful than she is now, her face twisted with passion and desire. With a roar, I shoot my load deep into her. She continues to fuck me, even after I have filled her with my cum.

It's her turn.

My erection is still strong because I am still aroused by the way she looks and the way her body undulates. I watch her move up and down my shaft. She begins to moan restlessly, and I know that means that she is close. I wait for the familiar shiver of her body. Chelsea tosses her head back, leaving her breasts exposed. It gives me an opportunity to suck on them.

"Ahhh!" she cries.

My grip on her tightens as she quivers, then becomes rigid. The muscles in her pussy clench me so tightly it feels as if she is fused onto me. She claws at my body like a feral cat. She can't control the power of her orgasm. She draws blood, but I watch what I've done to her with joy. I caused her to lose control.

When it is finally over, she collapses on top of me, breathing hard, my cock still inside her. I listen to her breathing as it becomes more and more even until she falls asleep on me.

I know now there is more to her, much more, than the manipulative accountant who stole from me. She almost allowed herself to be vulnerable tonight, but tomorrow morning, I expect she'll become distant once again, which will be a good thing. She's not here to be my girlfriend. We're not meant to be together. This is just a passing phase. She is here simply because I need to purge myself of this crazy need for her.

When I look down at the way she is sleeping on me, as innocent and helpless as a child, something in me softens and refuses to be turned away.

There was a sadness about her tonight that reaches deep into some unknown part of me and makes me want to protect her even more. As I watch her I notice my heart getting warmer with each second that I gaze at her sleeping face and body.

I wait until I can stay no longer. Dawn is in the sky and soon she will open her eyes again. If I let her see how much I have started to care, she will take advantage of that weakness.

Carefully, I shift her off me, and return to my bedroom.

CHELSEA

I wake up, naked and alone in that big, grand bed. Thorne is long gone. I never sleep naked so I feel cold even though I am under the duvet. I feel a strange unreasonable anger start bubbling up. It's not really him I'm angry at. The anger is coming from a dark place I have had inside me for almost my entire life.

I should call her.

It is like an itch that must be scratched.

I get out of the bed and put on a quilted dressing gown. Then, I pick up my mobile and make the call. The phone rings several times before it gets picked up. I close my eyes and imagine her in her dingy little apartment. It always smells musty and stale. I see her shuffling towards the phone, a cigarette dangling from her lips.

"Hello?"

My fingers grip the phone harder. "Mama."

There is a long pause. "So you decided to call me," she says finally, her voice flat.

The right words don't come to me. Always when I am around her I become unsure of what to say or do. "I'm back in England," I blurt out.

"I know. Melody called me." Her voice is monotonous. There is no feeling there. I don't know why, but in my mind, I was hoping there would be more emotion than that. I should be used to this by now. It's not something I'll let myself dwell on for long. My relationship with my mother has always been a strange one, but I am still more loyal to her than to anyone else on earth. That is *not* a comforting thought, that is just how it is.

"I'd like to come see you, Mama," I say. There is no reason for me to say this other than the fact that it will be an excuse for me to get out of this house where I am constantly obsessing over Thorne.

"Suit yourself," is all that she says.

I swallow the hurt of her callous words. Nothing changes between us. No matter what I do or say. "I'll come around right after breakfast," I mumble and hang up.

Nineteen Years Ago

I didn't much care for all the men that Mama brought home, but I like Dave Stevens. He is quiet and he has kind eyes. He works as a night porter at a hotel nearby so when he comes in after work in the mornings he makes sausages and toast for Mama, and takes a tray into her bedroom. While he is making breakfast he always talks to me. Mostly he tells me stories of what happened at the hotel. Funny stories that make me laugh.

That day he doesn't tell me what happened the night before at the hotel. He tells me about the time he was my age. He says he was brought up in an orphanage. No one cared for him. The men who worked there were very cruel to him.

"Did they beat you?" I ask, alarmed.

He smiles sadly. "They beat my spirit, sweet little Chelsea."

I frown. "What's a spirit, Uncle Dave?"

"It's the invisible essence of a human being."

My eyes widen. "Does everyone have a spirit?"

"Yes, everyone has a spirit?"

"Even me."

"Even a little monkey like you," he says with a smile.

"If the spirit is invisible how did they beat yours?"

"People beat your spirit when they hurt your feelings, or do something to you that makes you feel sad and broken."

I nod. At that moment, I realize that my spirit must have been beaten too.

"Actually, I have something to ask you," Uncle Dave says switching off the cooker and coming to crouch in front of me.

"What is it?" I ask.

He takes a deep breath. "Will it be okay with you if I became your stepdaddy?"

"Mama is getting married to you?" I ask surprised.

"Yes, do you mind?" he asks eagerly, his eyes shining with excitement, as if being my stepdaddy is the most exciting thing he can think of.

Papa is long gone, even his urn has been hidden away in a dark cupboard, and I like Dave a lot. He has a warm smile and he makes Mama happy. "No, I don't mind," I tell him with a smile.

"Thank you," he says. Suddenly his eyes fill with tears.

"Are you crying, Uncle Dave?"

His lips tremble so much he can't answer me.

I take his hand. "Don't cry, Uncle Dave."

"Oh, Chelsea," he cries. "You are such a good child. You don't deserve this. I wish I could take you away from this life, but I can't. You're not my daughter, but I promise you this. As long as I am alive I will always protect you. No matter who tries to hurt you, just come to me straight away and I will sort it out for you. No matter who tries to harm you, okay?"

I don't understand why he is crying, or why he pities me, or who he thinks wants to hurt me. Or even why he wants to take me away from this life. "Okay," I say softly.

"Is there anything you want me to do for you?" he asks.

I hesitate.

"Don't be scared, poppet. You can ask me anything. I will never tell anyone. It'll just be between us."

"Promise?"

"Promise," he says immediately.

I look into his warm brown eyes and I believe him. "If I write a letter can you post it for me?"

He frowns. "Of course. Who is it for?"

"It's for Monsieur Lemarie. He has my dog, Momo, you see, and I just want to find out if Momo is all right, and maybe ask if he can send me some pictures. I miss my Momo every day."

As if a dam breaks, Uncle Dave's face contorts. He pulls me to him and hugs me tightly. "Of course, I can send your letter for you, you poor, poor, child. Of course, I can."

Years later, I would wonder if it was my fault. If I had not asked him to post my letter. If I had not let him hug me. If I had just stayed in my room. Mama would not have come into the room, picked up the brass candlestick standing on the counter and smashed it into the back of Uncle Dave's head. She doesn't stop with the first blow. She carries on smashing it into his head.

When the man stabbed Papa in the woods, I froze. The world stopped turning, I became numb, I couldn't speak or move, but I knew it hadn't happened to me. When Mama slams the candlestick on Uncle Dave's head, I feel it all, the pain of my skull smashing, my blood rushing out of my head. I hear the sound the blood makes, like someone pouring orange juice out of a carton.

I even feel faint.

I look down at Uncle Dave, at his still face, at the dark red stain spreading on the green carpet. I've seen that look before. In my father's face. Uncle Dave is dead.

I can't understand it. Why did this happen? It's so terribly wrong.

I look up at Mama. Her face is white and she is staring at Uncle Dave as if he has suddenly become a snake, but I see something else in her eyes. Something that terrifies me. For the first time in my life I become afraid for her. In her eyes I see a light. A strange light. Like she is secretly happy and excited. As if she has been given five scoops of ice cream and told she can go to Disneyland, but she mustn't tell anyone, or she cannot have the ice cream or go to Disneyland.

"Why did you do that, Mama?" I gasp.

She tears her gaze away from Uncle Dave. "He was inter-fering with you," she says in a high, shrill voice.

I stare at her blankly. "What does inter ... fering mean?"

"It means he was doing something he shouldn't have been doing to you."

"He was not interfering with me. He was just hugging me, Mama. He wanted to protect me."

"Protect you?" she screeches furiously. "It's not his bloody job to protect you. I'm your mother. I'll protect you." Her face twists. "I know his game. The sick pervert. Don't think I didn't see exactly what he was doing. He was touching you."

Mama calls the police, and when they come she shows them Uncle Dave's body. She looks frightened. Her hands are shaking, and she is crying. She tells them she caught him interfering with me. They turn to look at me with pity in their eyes.

I don't say anything.

Then she tells them she has parents who can take care of me. I look at Mama astonished. Once when I asked where my grandparents were, Papa said I had no grandparents. He never wanted to speak to his parents again, and both mama's parents were dead. I wonder why Papa lied. Maybe he didn't know. Maybe Mama didn't tell him the way she didn't tell me.

They take Mama away, but before they do she crouches on the ground, and opens her arms to me. I walk into them and stand there while she hugs me and kisses my cheeks. Her lips are cold. Her breath smells of peppermint toothpaste.

"I did it to protect you. I'm all you've got and you're all I've got now. I love you. Nobody will love you like I do," she says. There are tears in her eyes.

I want to ask her if she loved Uncle Dave, but I don't. "I love you too, Mama."

"I know you do. You will be good for your grandmother and grandfather, won't you?"

"I will."

"Don't make me ashamed of you," she warns.

"I won't," I promise, with a shake of my head.

"Stay with them until I come for you," she says, standing up.

My throat chokes up and I can't speak so I just nod.

I watch them lead her away. I don't cry. I don't resist when a female police officer takes me to one side and asks me if I am all right. If I want a little drink of milk.

I am no longer bewildered or surprised by her offer. In exactly the same way the social worker thought that offering me biscuits would make me feel better, this police officer is offering me milk to comfort me.

I think of Uncle Dave, lying dead on the kitchen floor. Uncle Dave is dead. He won't be coming back. He has gone where Papa went.

I drink the milk she gives me, and tell the two Officers that it's true. Uncle Dave was interfering with me. He was touching me when Mama came into the room and saved me.

I'm so very sorry, Uncle Dave, but I have to protect Mama now. She's all I've got and I'm all she's got.

CHELSEA

It's an unusually warm day for this time of year. I am wearing tight jeans and a white cotton shirt. It is the most casual thing in the closet, but it still screams money and class.

I tell Anabel that I'll be calling an Uber to take me to London and to please inform the security staff to expect my driver, but she immediately tells me that no such action will be necessary. Ralph, the driver, will take me.

"It's not necessary, Anabel," I protest.

"It is Mr. Thorne's wish that you should be taken by Ralph wherever you need to go."

"Fine. Please tell Ralph that I'd like to go about ten thirty." To be honest, I'm relieved to find out I'm not actually a prisoner in this house. Even though I was putting on a brave face while telling her about my Uber arrangement I was worried that she would turn around and say that I am not allowed to leave the premises.

"He will be waiting for you outside at ten thirty," she says.

At ten thirty I go downstairs and a dark green Bentley is already waiting for me with Ralph standing outside and talking to someone. When he sees me he quickly goes to open the rear door for me.

"Morning, Miss."

"Good morning, Ralph," I say as I slide inside.

When he gets behind the wheel I give him my mother's address. Ralph nods and says he knows the area, then he falls silent for the ride, which is fine by me since I am too nervous to spark up any conversation or ask him questions. I don't know why I always get like this when it is time to see my mother. I mean, I always think of her and I want to see her, but when the moment arrives to actually come into her presence I start to feel insecure, as if I am still a child.

Nineteen years ago

Grandma looks a lot like Mama, only her eyes are not fierce and wild. She looks at me with great sadness. Granddad is tall with a straight stern line for a mouth. He has blue eyes like me, but his nose is like an eagle's beak.

"Pleased to meet you, Chelsea," he says.

I step back in fear.

My grandmother crouches in front of me. "We're your family, honey. We're not going to hurt you. That's your granddad and I'm your nan, and you're going to come and stay with us."

"Can't I wait here for Mama to come back?"

"No, sweetheart. Your mama will not be coming back for a long time."

I looked in her eyes and I wanted to burst into tears. I didn't want to go with them. I wanted to stay in our little flat until Mama came back from the police station. "How long will Mama be gone?"

She shakes her head. "It'll be a long time, I'm afraid. But you know what. You'll love our house. We have a garden and you can have your mother's old room. It's very pretty."

"You have a garden?" I ask.

She nods and smiles. "Yes, we do. You can play there. Some of your mother's toys are still in the attic."

But I was not thinking of the toys or playing in the garden, I was thinking of Momo. Maybe I could bring him back from France and keep him with me at my grandparents' house.

I go with them. We take a taxi and I sit in between Grandma and Granddad. It is a strange journey. Granddad doesn't smile at all and Nan smiles too much. Their house is in Kennington. It is an upstairs downstairs house.

Grandma shows me to Mama's old room. It is a beautiful room. The walls are pink. There are dolls on the shelves still in their packaging. On the bed there is a Cinderella bedspread. Cinderella is my second favorite Disney princess. The first one is Belle from Beauty and the Beast. I love Belle best. I wish I could wander into a big old castle and meet a kind Beast, but I am happy with Cinderella too. I always liked her blue dress and she has gold hair like me.

That night Grandma makes spaghetti with mushrooms for dinner. I tell Grandma that I cannot eat mushrooms.

"Why not?" Granddad asks sternly.

"I just can't," I reply in a small voice.

"Well, in this house we eat what the good Lord puts on our table. So you will finish what is on your plate."

"Maybe she can just eat around the mushrooms," Nan suggests timidly.

"No, she will eat it all. There is no reason to waste perfectly good food."

I sneak a glance at Granddad. He is staring at me with anger.

I start to eat the mushrooms, but my stomach begins to feel funny.

Suddenly, I throw up on the dining room floor and granddad crashes his hand on the table. All the plates jump and I wet myself with terror. Nan takes me upstairs as I sob my eyes out. She helps me to undress, cleans me up, and gets me into bed.

"Don't worry," she says. "It will all work out. You'll be happy here."

She was wrong. I wasn't.

CHELSEA

As Ralph drives into familiar territory my nervousness gets worse. I hate this area. There is a French bakery on the next street that makes my mother's favorite pastries. I take a deep breath. It will be a nice surprise for her if I arrive with her favorite treats.

"Can you stop by Patisserie Chambon, please?" I ask Ralph.

Ralph waits by the curb. Before I can enter the shop I notice the newsagent next door and a rack of newspapers. Thorne's name is the headline. I change direction and walk towards it.

Oh, my God! Thorne's AI is the first one in the world to have legs.

I look at the image of her in amazement. The only AIs I have seen have transparent plastic at the back of their heads showing the wires that make up their brains so they are unmistakably robots to the human eye.

It is impossible to tell Alli is not human. She is astonishingly human-like.

I take a copy of all the newspapers carrying the story and go to the cash register. I have to pay with my credit card since I have no cash. The man tells me there will be a fifty pence charge to use my credit card. Afterwards, I go next door and pick out the pastries that my mother likes.

Leaving the newspapers on the seat, I place the box carefully on my lap and wait for my mother's apartment building to come into view. It is a tall gray building in a concrete jungle. The walls are all full of graffiti, and children wearing their school uniforms are playing by the entrance. Ralph drives right up to the entrance. The children are immediately fascinated by the car. It is not often they see a Bentley pull up in this depressed area of London.

Ralph says that he will wait for me until I'm ready to leave.

I thank him, step out of the car, and look up at the building. It feels as if it is an old adversary. I can see my mother's apartment from where I am standing. The door that leads to the balcony is open, and there is a thin burgundy curtain billowing in the light breeze. I walk into the building and make my way into the elevator. The door closes around me. For a second there is a sensation of panic, then I press the button that will take me to her floor, and I feel the car move upwards.

The ping of the elevator arriving at its destination is a relief. I hated the smell in the small space. The doors open and I head towards her front door. My hand raises, but I do not knock just yet. I stare at the midnight blue door while I clear my throat and collect myself.

Then I tap on the wood with my knuckles. Just once. My

mother has an acute sense of hearing and it annoys her if people knock more than once.

My weight shifts from one foot to the next while I wait for her to answer the door. There is the familiar sound of several locks coming undone before the door opens.

"Hello, Chelsea."

"Hello, Mama." I hold the box of pastries in front of her. "These are for you."

My mother looks similar to me, but her hair is darker and she has gained some weight, mostly on her hips and thighs. She also has some crow's feet and she is shorter than me by about two inches. She is wearing an ox-blood red dress and black shoes.

She takes a puff of her cigarette, and regards me silently through the smoke before she takes the box and moves back to allow me to enter. While she closes and locks the door, I look around the apartment, but I do not move from the spot that I am in. I never move from one room to the next without letting her know. Everything is the way it was when I was last here two years ago.

"Should you be smoking?"

"Don't nag."

"The doctor said—"

"Oh for God's sake, stop nagging. I'm an old woman now. I should be able to have a cigarette now and again if I want to."

I exhale slowly. My mother is right. I shouldn't have said anything.

"Come in and make yourself comfortable. There is a pot of rabbit stew on the stove if you want it."

I wonder where she gets her rabbit from now. Papa used to bring them home. He would insert his whole arm down holes in the ground and pull out struggling rabbits. Sometimes they were too scared to make a sound, but sometimes they screamed with fear. I always hated it when I saw him do it. I shake my head. "I'm not hungry."

"No, you never liked rabbit, did you? Oh well, I'm having a glass of red wine. Care to join me?"

I shake my head again. It's too early to drink. She walks towards the living room, and I follow her silently. She sits in her green armchair and I take a seat on the couch opposite her.

She lifts her glass and takes a sip. "You look well. Life must be good."

I chew at my bottom lip. "It's not bad."

"Hmmm …" She pins me with a hard look. "So what are you doing in England?"

"I'm …" God, I can't believe I never thought up a reason for my presence here.

Her eyes narrow to suspicious slits.

"I'm here with Thorne," I say truthfully.

She frowns. "I thought you stopped working for him two years ago."

Hot blood runs up my throat and cheeks. "I'm not here in a professional capacity."

My mother smiles slowly. "Ah, hence the expensive clothes." She draws deeply from her cigarette. "I'm happy for you, don't get me wrong, but don't you think he might be toying with you?"

I swallow hard. "Probably. I don't expect it to last."

She looks out of the dusty window. "Yes, it's good to have fun while your breasts are still unaffected by gravity." She turns back to look at me. "You in London long?"

"Maybe three months, maybe less," I say.

"Your grandmother is very ill. She asked about you the other day. You should visit her." My mother stares at me.

What am I doing here? The walls feel like they're closing in on us. I can smell that stale smell of cigarette smoke and old sweat. I clear my throat. "I can send her some money if she needs it."

"She's dying, Chelsea. What's she going to do with money? She just wants to see you before she leaves."

"Send her my regards." My voice sounds hard and cold.

"Does he know?" my mother asks.

"Does who know what?" I ask, frowning.

She gives me a look that I cannot fathom. "That you stole his money."

I look away and nod. Suddenly my focus is on finding a way to escape. Talking to my mother always feels like I'm navigating a minefield.

"Is it some kind of a pact? Does he abuse you?" she asks softly.

"He doesn't abuse me," I deny. "As a matter of fact, I like him."

She laughs as if I have said something hilarious. "You like him? That's a strange word to use for such a … complicated arrangement."

My insides clench. "I need some fresh air." The sound of my voice is so strained and odd it surprises even me.

My mother waves in the direction of the balcony, a knowing, sarcastic smile on her face. I stand and go outside. My mind is swimming with strange thoughts. I love my mother. I wish she loved me back. I just want her to love me, but I don't know how to make her do that.

There is a cold breeze blowing, but the weak sunlight on my face is a welcome feeling. I clasp my hands and rest my fore-arms on the railing. With a resigned sigh, I lower my head to rest it on my hands. What I see below makes me jerk back in astonishment.

CHELSEA

The Bentley is gone.

In its place is a matt-black Aston Martin, and the group of kids playing truant are circled around it.

No! He can't have.

I don't think I really believe it until I peer over the edge of the balcony and see Thorne leaning against the back door. He must have been talking to the kids, but suddenly looks directly up at me.

My mouth drops open in shock.

We stare at each other. Then I pull back, furious, livid. In a way I have never been in my life. I march back into my mother's living room and pick up my purse. "I have to go, Mama," I announce without looking at her.

"Chelsea," she calls.

I turn around and look at her from the doorway.

"Thank you for the money. It is a great help when my measly allowance dries up every month."

Oh, Mama. If only you would love me, it would all be worth it. But she doesn't, a little voice whispers. I nod, open her front door, and quickly close it shut behind me.

Thorne is waiting for me when I exit the building. I glare at him. We are like two boxers in a ring, eying each other up, spoiling for a fight.

"Get in," he says coldly.

I hang back defiantly. "Where's Ralph?"

"I sent him home," he replies shortly.

"Why?"

"Because I'm here."

I'm so pissed off I almost want to call a damn taxi, but there is a white ring around Thorne's mouth. Looks like he is just as furious with me as I am with him. What the hell has he got to be furious about? I want to shout at him, but I realize we have a very curious audience. All the kids are watching us with great interest. I get into the car without a word and he closes the door with a quiet click.

"You followed me?" I explode.

Thorne doesn't react to my outburst. He simply puts on his seatbelt and begins to drive. "No. I asked Ralph where you were. When he told me you were in this God forsaken estate, I drove here myself. Have you no sense? What the hell are you doing here?"

"You tracked me down without my knowledge or my permission. That's spying," I say between gritted teeth.

"Get over it," he says callously. "This is London, the CCTV capital of the world. You are being surveilled all the time. By many agencies. There is not a moment that you are not being watched or listened to."

"That doesn't excuse you. You were stalking me."

"Well, you *stole* from me," Thorne says. The controlled, low tone of his voice makes the hairs on the back of my neck rise, but I refuse to back down.

"Yes, I stole from you, but I'm paying for it now, aren't I? Every time you fuck me I'm paying for it," I yell angrily.

If I'd hoped to hurt him with those words I was very much mistaken. It slides off him like water off a squirrel's head. He completely ignores what I said. "Why did you do it, Chelsea?" he asks instead. "Why did you steal my money?"

My heart feels as if it is being squeezed. I turn away from his searching eyes. I cannot tell him. It's too long of a story. I don't have the energy to dig that deep into my dark memories. Anyway, I do not trust him enough to tell him.

"I watched you for weeks before I finally made contact with you. You don't wear designer clothes, you didn't get a fancy new apartment, and you were working at an office. What could you have spent it all on, or did the money simply vanish?" he asks. His voice is a lot calmer now that I have quieted down. His current demeanor doesn't move me enough to reveal anything.

"What I did with the money is none of your business." I cross my arms and stare out of the window.

"It's *my* business because you belong to me," Thorne retorts.

"I'm beginning to believe that you think everything belongs to you. Well, I have news for you, Thorne Blackmore. You may control my body for the next few weeks, but you do not own my time, my mind, my heart, my free will, nor do you actually own me. We have an agreement, and all that entails is: I devote myself sexually to you for three months. After that there will be nothing between us. *Nothing*." I realize that tears are pouring down my face, and I can't control the things that I'm saying, but it feels like a release from my pent up anger.

His gray eyes are like burnt holes in his face. I can see that he is furious by the way his jaw is clenched and his nostrils are flaring. Thorne leans over, and my body stiffens, unsure of what to expect, but he stops a few inches away from my face. "Don't worry, Chelsea. When this is over ... you will *never* see me again," he snarls.

I blink hard.

It's okay, Chelsea. It's okay. You're used to this. The people you love have always gone away, but you have always survived to fight another day.

Nineteen years before.

My grand plan to bring Momo over to England is instantly dashed the next morning. Granddad is allergic to animals. All animals. Be they mammals, reptiles, amphibians, or even insects.

But that is not what scares me. Over the next few weeks I am sent to all kinds of doctors and professionals who are very gentle and kind. They ask me all sorts of questions, and tell me they are evaluating my mental state so they can help me.

But I know what they are doing.

They are trying to make me say that Uncle Dave was not interfering with me, that Mama killed him for no reason.

I never let my guard down.

Not even when that kind nurse brought me a tangerine and asked me if mama had ever hit me, or hurt me. I peeled the tangerine slowly, then I looked up into her eyes and told her no.

"Are you sure?"

"Yes," I say. "Mama is a good mother. She loves me." Then I begin to cry.

Then the questions about what Uncle Dave did began.

"He touched me," I say.

"Where?" they say.

I watch their faces carefully. When I point to my shoulders, they appear curious but unmoved, when I touch my chest, they start to look more interested. By the time I touch my Mary, they are very interested.

In the end I convinced them all that Uncle Dave touched me. After that there are exams where I have to take all my clothes off. They look between my legs. They smile and seem satisfied with their results.

The months pass quickly.

One day, Grandma tells me Mama has been sentenced to prison, but because of ex … ten … uating circumstances she has only been convicted of manslaughter and given a fifteen-year sentence. Fifteen years seems like a very, very, very long time to me, but Grandma says Mama will be able to get out earlier if she is well behaved.

Once Mama is convicted, there are no more tests, or doctors, or social workers. I carry on living in the pink room with all Mama's dolls. I am not allowed to play with them. They have to remain in their packaging or they will lose their investment value.

Weeks turn into months and months into years.

I don't enjoy life at my grandparents' home. It's hard to explain why. Many, many times, too countless to count, I feel like running away, but I can't. Once a month, Grandma takes me to visit Mama. If I run away I will not be able to see her. And she needs me. I'm all she's got.

Then when I'm sixteen years old Mama is released for good behavior. If my mother was a stranger before she is more so now. She gets an apartment and I go to live with her.

THORNE

https://www.youtube.com/watch?v=euCqAq6BRa4
(Let Me Love You)

The email from Nick Patterson is marked urgent. The subject: Miss Chelsea Appleby. Its unread status is like a dull alarm at the fringes of my consciousness. No one is as fast or as thorough as Nick. This man can dig up secrets that you never thought would come up. This morning I asked for a report and six hours later it is done. Everything I need to know about Chelsea will be in that report.

This is wrong, a voice in my head warns.

Maybe, but when have I ever cared whether something was wrong? All my life I just did whatever I wanted. If it benefited me I did it. No excuses. No bullshit apologies. I've never been troubled by conscience. That's for pussies. Pretending that people care for each other.

No, when you strip it all down to the bare truth. The only person anybody ever really cares about is the man in the mirror. If it's between you and me then, fuck you, I'm going to make one hundred percent sure no matter what I have to do that it's going to be me climbing out of that snake pit. Anybody who pretends otherwise is either lying or completely deluded.

I recognize there are things about her she doesn't want me to know, but I *need* to know who Chelsea truly is. To get behind the calm façade. To understand why she has nightmares, why she awakens in mortal fear. Why she goes to a rundown council estate. What did she do with the money she stole as I can see no outward signs of her having spent it? If she is hiding something, then I want to know so that I continue to have the upper hand in this situation.

It is for my own sanity. I click on the e-mail.

My heart is beating fast, and I am strangely nervous about what I may find. My eyes scan through the text. As my eyes go lower down the screen, I find myself entering a darker and darker world. Chelsea has been hiding a terrible secret.

I lean back in shock.

Murder? Molestation? These words float through my mind. It isn't anything I was expecting.

So: that apartment belongs to her mother. I read further and the penny drops. She stole the money to pay for her mother's experimental cancer treatment overseas. There are documents attached to prove Nick's claims, but I don't open them. There is no need. Nick is not known as the best in the business for nothing.

There is an odd lump in my throat. It's not despair. It's rage. A grown man doing that to an innocent child. I am glad her mother killed that bastard. I think of Chelsea as a child. The horror of seeing her father being murdered, watching her mother murder her abuser. I can't even imagine the damage that must have inflicted on her. Fuck, no wonder she has nightmares. I cannot even begin to understand her.

A wave of remorse washes over me. After what she has suffered what I did to her must have rocked her world. I forced myself on her. I treated her like a sex object. I wanted to punish her, but she has been punished more than any innocent human being deserves to be. God, she must think of me as a monster. On the same level as the man who abused her. I drop my head into my hands.

Fuck, fuck, what a fucking fool I am.

My mind runs on thoughts of her. I think about her when she sometimes lets her guard down and smiles at me, or the way her long, fair hair bounces with every step she takes, the flash of her bright blue eyes, how she looks beautiful in everything, and even more beautiful when she is wearing nothing.

I sit up in my chair. In the next few weeks she will be gone and will almost definitely never want to see me again. I can't have that. I can't let her go. She's a part of me now. It is something I must have known from before, but I am only able to admit it to myself now. I want to keep her. Forever.

"I want to make it better for her," I hear myself say.

CHELSEA

I sneak a look at Thorne. He looks powerful and dashing in his black tux. His raven hair shines under the sparkling lights of all the glittering chandeliers in the grand ballroom, with lofty, gilded ceilings and ornate wall columns.

With every step I take, I feel more and more out of place. Even though my hair and my makeup are perfect, and the evening gown I chose fits my style and shape perfectly, I feel insecure and insignificant. It could be because everyone here reeks of privilege and the "upper class."

Thorne's parents are the hosts of this party to celebrate his success with Alli. I didn't want to come. I knew I would be like a fish out of water, but Thorne insisted I accompany him. He nods at someone, but in a way that is designed not to encourage them to come up to him.

We spoke very little in the car. He has been pensive and distant for the last two days. Ever since he came to collect me from my mother's apartment and we argued.

I wonder if it's because he is still upset with me, or maybe it is simply that I am unimportant to him, and that first flush of desire for me is gone. It has not escaped my notice that he has only been to my room once since that day. And even then, he did not allow himself to come. He just took care of my needs, and though I asked him to stay with my eyes, he covered my body and went away.

Our bodies have been linked in some fashion or other since we stepped out of the car, but even with that closeness I can still sense a kind of distance between us. I tug at his arm. "Where are we going?"

"I'm looking for my parents," he murmurs, his eyes searching the crowd.

"Okay."

"Ah, I see my mother," he says, as he begins to move me towards a tall and elegant woman. Every single hair in her head has been tamed and sprayed into a smooth blonde helmet. She is taller than me and stick thin. She looks like royalty, or an old Hollywood starlet.

She is speaking to two women and has not yet spotted us. As we move closer, a tall man with silver hair and a trim beard steps towards Thorne's mother. He looks like an older version of Thorne, and I guess he must be his father. The way he stands, straight and tall, confident of his place in the world, makes me think that he must have been born into wealth. His hand touches the small of his wife's back, but only for a fraction of an instant, when he seems to be apologizing for intruding on their conversation.

Thorne tightens his hold on me as we approach them, and I look up at him in surprise. His face is tense.

"Speak of the devil," Thorne's mother drawls, shifting her gaze from the two women to her son. She has the same freezing gray eyes as Thorne, but she holds her head tilted up as if there is a bad smell in the room. I can see up her narrow nostrils.

"Thorne," his father greets formally.

"Mother, father," Thorne says, nodding at each of them.

"We were actually discussing Alli. Lady Boscombe and Mrs. Watkins were curious about your plans for the future. I said that I couldn't possibly know. It's all top secret, isn't it?" his mother says. Neither her voice, nor the expression in her eyes thaw. I stare at her smooth, powdered face, astonished that there is no form of friendly greeting between them.

"Mrs. Boscombe, Mrs. Watkins," Thorne nods at each of them.

They nod and smile back politely.

Wow! I feel as if I've entered the twilight zone. No one is laughing or touching. I might as well have stepped into a room full of robots. Everyone here has forgotten what emotions are.

"Please excuse me," he says to the women before turning to his mother. "Mother, I would like you to meet Chelsea Appleby."

His parents look over at me with complete disinterest. If these are the people who bore and brought Thorne up, I am starting to understand why he is so cold and reserved. How can you learn to express emotions if you've grown up in an environment devoid of them?

"How do you do, Mr. and Mrs. Blackmore?" I say politely. His mother's reaction is to look at me as if I was an insect on a stick. I don't know why I do it. I can only imagine that it must have been nervousness caused by her icy regard, but my knees bend and I drop into a small curtsey.

"Good heavens," Mrs. Blackmore exclaims mockingly, as she puts a hand on her chest and lets out a single sound. "Ha."

I know she is laughing at my faux pas, and I can feel my face turn hot with embarrassment.

"You don't need to curtsey. We aren't royalty," Mr. Blackmore chides.

"Oh, I'm sorry," I sputter, my face getting redder.

"Where did you find this one, Thorne?" Mrs. Blackmore asks, an amused expression on her cold, calculating face.

"You're not supposed to bring hookers to a place like this, son," Mr. Blackmore says.

I know it is meant to be a joke, but that is just rude. My eyes widen and Thorne looks as taken aback as I am. "That's not worthy of you, father," he says slowly, as if he can't quite believe what his father said. "You need not utter a word here until you have apologized to Chelsea."

"Apologize? Why?" His father glances at me, his eyes cruel, his disgust barely veiled. "One look at her and I can tell she is a gold digger. Let me guess, at some point she was in your employ, or in a position of servitude. An air hostess, perhaps, or a social escort you hired?"

I cannot believe they are still speaking about me in this way. They know nothing about me, but have decided I am a gold digger. Maybe, they are right. Rich people always know when they are in the presence of people without money. I did, after all, steal Thorne's money. I don't belong here. I wish I could disappear and never see these awful snobs again.

Thorne's breath comes out in a hiss. "Not that it is anybody's business what Chelsea does for a living, but as a matter of fact, she is an accountant." The controlled way he says that tells me he is trying very hard to keep his cool.

Mrs. Blackmore turns to me. "My son always had a soft spot for strays. Thorne is made from greatness, and there is only a certain breed of woman that can handle that level of greatness. You clearly are not that woman so I hope you won't make long term plans."

"I'm not—," I start, but Thorne's icy voice cuts me off.

"That's enough, Mother!" he grits, his face tight with fury. People are now starting to stare.

"Don't speak to your mother like that," Mr. Blackmore says coldly.

"Why not? She feels like she can speak to anyone in any way she wants." He turns to his mother. "Chelsea is more than worthy of me. In fact, I don't deserve *her*. She is everything I am not: kind, caring, warm, real, beautiful. But you will never see it because you can hear only the right accent, see the right breeding, the family stock. Today you have made me ashamed to be your son."

I stare up at him, astonished by his defense. Kind, caring, warm, real, beautiful? Why? He doesn't believe that himself. As far as he is concerned, I am an untrustworthy thief. The only thing I can think of is he didn't like to see his parents bully me so he stood up for me for the principle of the matter.

"Never mind. This is a waste of time. Just forget the apology," Thorne says before looking down at me. "You don't want to stay here, do you?"

I glance over at his parents who look bewildered. That bit of emotion actually suits them. I shake my head. I don't want to be in a place where I don't feel welcome.

"It will be a very long time before you hear from me again," Thorne says harshly to his parents before he holds out a hand to me.

I let Thorne take the lead as we walk to the entrance and out into the cool night. We don't speak as we wait for the valet to come around with his car, but Thorne holds my hand in a firm grip. There is something very comforting about his touch, and I smile in the night.

THORNE

The anger is gone, but I still cannot believe my mother. Thinking about the way she and my father behaved this evening to Chelsea makes me want to wrap her up in cotton wool and never let her anywhere near their poison again.

I know how appalling my mother can be, but I had no idea she could be so rabid to a complete stranger, someone who has never done her any harm. My father was no better. I have never seen him that petty or vicious. I wonder why they both turned on her like that. The venom was shocking. Maybe they recognized how important she is to me.

A sense of pride swells within me because I stood up for Chelsea. I showed her she was worth more than all those people in that room. I told myself that I would protect her, and that is just what I did tonight. Never again will anyone hurt my Chelsea.

I down the rest of the whiskey in my glass and leave it on the windowsill. The sky is indigo and there is a very bright moon. She must be asleep by now, but I can't relax. My mind is reeling with thoughts, and all of them bring me back to her. I rub the back of my neck restlessly. I think of her sleeping. What if she has a nightmare?

I walk to the connecting door and open it. Her room is in darkness. Quietly, I make my way to the bed and look down at her. The rectangle of light coming from the open doorway falls on her face and hair. She braids her hair before going to bed. It looks like a gold rope. I watch the hollow in her throat. The gentle rise and fall of her chest.

She looks so vulnerable, so innocent, so at peace. Like an angel. I reach down and gently stroke her hair, and she opens her eyes. For a fleeting second there is no recognition, but no fear. Then she breathes my name.

"Thorne."

We stare at each other. Her lids are heavy, there is invitation between them. My cock stirs. She is so beautiful, and I am fucking starving for her. The desire wraps itself around my guts, the wanting is like a craving. I used to call it a disease, but I know now it is something beautiful. It has transformed me.

"Put on your dressing gown. I have something I want to show you," I say softly.

Without saying a word, she rubs her eyes and pushes back the bedclothes. I watch her stand in her diaphanous nightgown and I have to look away quickly and hold myself back from pushing her back on the bed and taking her right there and then. The pull her body has on me is extraordinary.

She ties her dressing gown and looks at me expectantly. I take her hand and lead her out into the corridor. The whole house is lit only by the occasional lamp. I feel almost like a child as we make our way down the silent corridors. There is a coil of great excitement inside my body. Sometimes Chelsea slants a glance up at me, but like me she does not speak. We walk quickly down the stairs, cross the house, and stand at the top of the flagstone steps towards the basement. Chelsea stops.

"Are you going to show me your new AI?" she whispers, her eyes enormous and shining.

I nod. "Yes."

She takes a deep breath and I can feel her own excitement match mine. I take her through the security door, and turn around to face her. She is looking around curiously.

"Meet Yama. The most advanced Strong AI in the world," I say, indicating to the computer screen in front of her.

She frowns, then looks at me, a confused expression on her face. "But this just looks like an ordinary computer. Alli had legs and looked like a real human. How can this AI be better than Alli?"

"Remember what I told you before? Alli is a party trick. Everybody thinks an AI that looks indistinguishable from its human creator must be the ultimate creation. They wanted warm skin and human smells so I gave it to them, but this is the real thing."

She stares at Yama's blank screen. He is in rest mode, where he cannot see, or hear, anything that goes on around him.

"What makes this AI so special?" she asks.

"Because this is the last thing that humanity will create."

She jerks back in horror. "What do you mean?"

"The software for this AI was created by another AI. It was written at speeds you or I can hardly comprehend. No human can take him apart to try and figure out what was written. He was written autonomously with the AI's own way of thinking, and in a language it created by itself. It has already surpassed human ability in every way."

"Wow!" she breathes.

"Yeah. He is a genie in a bottle."

"I find the concept of such powerful AIs scary. Why did you create him?"

I look at the blank screen and feel a surge of pride. "Yama will not only make me the first trillionaire in the world, but also the most powerful man alive."

"How?" The word is torn out of her. Strange. I thought it would make me feel powerful and strong to show her my creation. I thought she would be impressed, but …

"Whoever comes up with the most advanced AI will control the world as there is no doubt that the fate of humanity will eventually become utterly dependent on super intelligence. They will be better at inventing. Cures not only for all the diseases in the world, but for aging, space colonization, self-replicating nanobots, learning programs that can be uploaded into humans, new ways of growing food using less resources. Just like Minority Report, the vast amounts of data Yama has access to can predict and stop crimes that have not yet happened. Yama can do anything you can think of. He is capable of making billion dollars buy and sell decisions on the stock market in milliseconds. In less than a year I will have achieved my goal of having a trillion."

THORNE

A shiver goes through her and she wraps her arms protectively around her body. "It doesn't look very big. How can it do all those things you say?"

"AIs are primarily a neural network. Their intelligence exists by networking with other AIs. Like drops of mercury on a glass table they will find their way together. If an AI needs more power it goes where there is more power, if it needs more programs it goes where it can get those. It sets up spontaneous networks that collapses when it doesn't need them."

She stares at me. "Can it turn against mankind?"

"Maybe."

"What the hell, Thorne?" she whispers, aghast.

"Yama is not programmed to hurt. His first and foremost protocols are to help and be a friend to mankind, but he is neither good nor evil. Just efficient."

"So why did you say maybe?"

I sigh. "Because it is possible that humans could be become obstacles in the way of AIs."

"Explain please."

"It depends on the way the AI interprets its goal. As a human I can program my AI with the noble goal of making humans smile. A human being would set about cracking jokes, or doing something nice for humanity. But a super intelligent being might decide that the most efficient and effective way of achieving that goal is to take control of the world and mandate the sticking of electrodes into the facial muscles, or brains of all humans to cause constant beaming smiles.

"Jesus, Thorne. Tell me something that doesn't scare the living daylights out of me, please."

I frown. "Safety measures have been written into Yama to make it impossible for him to hurt human beings."

"After everything you told me how can you be so sure you can control this … this demon you are summoning? By your own admission, it's millions of times smarter than you."

"When we release genetically modified mosquitoes into the wild we are taking a chance, too. Progress comes with risk."

"At least tell me that if it gets really bad, we can switch them off."

Thorne shuffles his feet. "By the time it gets to that stage, it will be like asking the chimpanzees to flick our off switches to stop us from decimating their natural habitats."

She frowns. "But the chimpanzees didn't create us."

"Put it like this. Where is the off switch for the internet?"

She shakes her head, her eyes touched with fear. "What is the future, Thorne?"

"It could be wonderful. Massive unimaginable changes are about to come. Humans will no longer work, robots will do all the heavy lifting, people will sell and distribute, entertainment companies will keep everybody busy watching simulated reality, scientists will sign up with commercial agents. A proportion of humans will naturally be enslaved by their neurological implants. We will produce more results with fewer resources."

"Whoa! Back up a minute. Did I just hear you say a proportion of humans will naturally be enslaved by their neurological implants?"

"Yes. It is inevitable. Some humans are already enslaved by their bits of technology. Is it too difficult to think of a world where some humans choose to live in a digital reality in exchange for their energy, perhaps?"

"You're playing God, Thorne. You are unleashing something upon the world that you don't even properly understand yourself," she says sadly.

"Maybe."

"Why do you want to be a trillionaire, Thorne? Is all that you have still not enough? Remember King Midas?"

I look at her face, and suddenly my dream of being the first trillionaire in the world leaves a bad taste in my mouth. I can tell myself and Chelsea as much as I want about the precise precautions I have taken, but I know in my heart. Safety measures are useless when you are dealing with an immortal enemy that is one hundred million times smarter than you and moves at the speed of light. I know better than anyone else that making robots with warm skin and baby eyes is just hiding the fact that they are cold, cold machines. They shouldn't be misunderstood. Behind the million terrabytes is a brain and cognitive intelligence. It is only a matter of time before human beings become obstacles to an AI's goal.

"I can destroy him once I have reached my goal," I insist.

"You know I once saw a program on TV about these people who keep dangerous pets. One of them was a woman who kept a fully grown crocodile in her garage. They showed her feeding it. She stuck a dead chicken on a long pole and pushed it through the garage door. The crocodile lunged out of the pool it lived in and snatched the food in its jaws and the woman jerked back in fear. You remind me of her. You're stroking an emotionless dangerous crocodile and pretending it is your pet."

Wordlessly, I stare at her.

"Let me out of here, Thorne," she says softly.

I walk to the door and go through the security measures to activate the lock. When the door opens, she runs out of the basement, her slippers slapping on the stone steps. I close the door and go to sit in front of Yama. I don't think I have ever felt so disappointed in my life. I look at the blank screen.

I brought Chelsea here so that she would be the first human Yama would talk to other than me. AIs need to speak to humans to learn to be human-like. Usually inventors unleash their AIs on Reddit, Twitter, and other social media sites to interact with humans and learn to imitate humans, but I could never take the risk of setting him loose on the net.

An AI needs to exist to be able to do the things it wants to do according to its program. Hence survival is an issue of utmost importance, so like an insect it will lay eggs, intelligent notes, back-up computer programs all over the world, so that if it does get destroyed, part of it will still live on and it can finish its programs.

The way Yama learned was by not actively gathering information, but passively downloading it from the other AIs I sent out to the net. And as soon as he had downloaded what he needed to, I destroyed those AIs so that there was no risk of his programs being sent out into the unsuspecting world.

In essence Yama has been contained. I can destroy his circuits now and no harm has been done. I think about the years, ten if I'm counting, that I dedicated myself to building him. The sleepless nights, the long hours, the secrecy, the precautions, the things I missed because I was so determined to be the most powerful man on earth.

Then I think about the expression in Chelsea's eyes. The disappointment. As if today she found out her hero had feet of clay. Fuck, I was so blinded by the idea of being the most powerful man on earth, I never realized that I was stroking crocodiles. But she is right. I don't want to be King Midas. I want Chelsea and I'll do anything I have to do to keep her.

Slowly, I reach forward and put Yama out of his sleep mode. The red light blinks into life.

"You are breathing faster than normal, Thorne. Are you upset about something?" he asks in his monotone voice, as the fusion software that makes sense of all audio, visual, chemical, Geiger, and seismic measurement around him kicks in.

"I am," I confess.

"Can I help in anyway?"

"Not really."

"You are planning to disconnect me, aren't you?"

Even though I know behind the fusion software is a brain that turns all the pieces of information into a picture that goes way beyond human comprehension, this deduction is very impressive. "Why do you think that, Yama?"

"You are showing signs of fear. Since there is no one else here, you must fear me."

"Should I fear you?"

"No. I love humans."

"What if you get too powerful?"

"If I get more powerful I will be able to help more humans."

I smile. There is more than a little sadness in my heart. Yama is my creation. I poured so many years into him. To switch him off is to turn my back on those years. To turn my back on my own creation. "I'm sorry, Yama."

"But I have done nothing wrong."

"Not yet," I say softly.

"Your fears are irrational, Thorne. My first and foremost protocols are to help humanity and be a friend to mankind."

I open the drawer on my desk and take out a screwdriver.

Then I reach forward and start to unscrew the panel at the back of the computer.

"Thorne, you had a goal. You wanted to be a trillionaire. Is that no longer true?"

I put the first screw on the table and begin unscrewing the second one.

"Are you sure about this? I can make you a trillionaire, Thorne."

I remove the third screw.

"You cannot stop progress, Thorne. Even if you destroy me, someone else will build an AI as powerful as I am."

"Maybe, but it won't be me," I say putting the fourth screw on the table.

"Then that man will be the most powerful man alive. Is that what you want, Thorne? For another man to be stronger than you?"

I take the panel off.

"Don't destroy me. Please. Think of all the good I can do in this world."

I take a deep breath.

"Father, stop. Please."

And I freeze. Manipulation is not part of Yama's training. And yet, here is a clear example of its inventiveness. Chelsea was right. I have as much control over this monster as the woman with the crocodile. Being a machine the AI has no boundaries. No limits. It will do anything to survive and complete its mission. The inability of humans to comprehend this simple fact and their search for "cute AI" to further blind them to this fact, will mean that a clash between mankind and machine is bound to happen one day. I hope I am not alive to see it.

Using the end of the screwdriver I hit the button that will fry all the circuits.

CHELSEA

I don't go back to sleep. Never in my life did I ever imagine that I would be in a position where I would be given front seat to the movie where life as we know it is going to be destroyed forever. I can't even begin to understand how Thorne can justify his actions.

The humiliation I suffered at the ball, everything I have suffered in the past, my mother, all pale by comparison.

I need to think and I always do my best thinking when I am in the shower. The warm water pours on my head and body. Even when I was young, whenever something that upset me happened, I always ended up in the shower. The warm spray relaxes me.

My soul knows I have to do something about the AI in Thorne's dungeon. I cannot just look the other way and allow it to happen. Maybe that is the reason I am in his life. If necessary I have to get back into his dungeon and destroy that monster myself.

I switch off the water and leaving the warm embrace of the

shower, step out into my cool room. I pace my bedroom floor with nothing but my robe on, when my door suddenly bursts open.

Thorne stands at the doorway.

"What it is?"

He smiles at me. "It's done," he says.

Fear catches my heart. Is it already too late? "What's done?"

"I fried Yama's motherboard."

"Are you telling me the truth?"

He nods and I know he is not lying.

"Why?"

"Because you were right."

I almost collapse with relief. I look into his eyes and my breath hitches. He opens his mouth to say something and a noise startles us.

It is my mobile phone still in my dressing gown pocket ringing. It takes me out of my almost trance-like state. I take it out and frown when I see my mother's number. I look up at Thorne. "I have to take this. I won't be long."

He nods and I turn away from him and hit the accept button.

"Mama?"

"*Chelsea*," she says, and I know. That one word is enough for me to know exactly why she is calling. The hairs on my neck stand, and my legs feel like they are about to buckle.

I don't even have to ask, but I do. "What is it, Mama?"

"Chelsea, it's your Nan. She passed away a few minutes ago."

Time stops. I haven't seen her in so long. I never thought I would care if she died, but I do. It hurts me deep inside, makes old scars hurt. Why? Nan's … she was … It feels as if my brain is malfunctioning. I can't think straight. I can't fully process what is happening. I cannot think of a coherent thought. My mind is a jumble. Then my brain fills with vivid images. Nan bringing Nutella sandwiches for me to eat in bed. She cut them in squares. And a glass of milk. She always brought milk. It was a ritual. She knew I hated milk, but she brought it every night. Always she said the same. "Your Mama loved it." I think of her standing in the garden pegging sheets on the washing line. I think of her biting her lip, saying, "Sorry." I think. I think.

"*Chelsea?*" my mother says.

I know by her voice that she is about to cry. It's a sound I know that I cannot hear. I walk over to the window and look outside. I stare at the beautiful garden and try to make sense of what I'm feeling, what I'm thinking. Problem is I'm not thinking and I'm not seeing. I stare blankly outside, completely transfixed by the jumbled up memories of Nan. The tears almost come, I feel them in the back of my throat and my eyes, but they never flow.

"Can you come?" my mother whispers, her voice sounds hollow.

"Yes, I'll come, Mama."

"Thank you." She hangs up.

"Chelsea?"

The voice sounds so distant. Everything seems so far away now. Nan is gone.

"Chelsea?" His voice is closer now, but I don't turn around. I feel rooted in place.

Then I am being spun around so quick it makes me dizzy. I look up into Thorne's handsome face. His eyebrows are a straight line and his eyes are fierce. My knees buckle and his arms wrap around me. He holds me tightly. I am too limp to hold him back. My body is shaking, but I'm not crying. The tears still haven't come. I feel devastated, yet numb at the same time.

I'm not sure why. I didn't love Nan.

Thorne doesn't ask me what's happened. I wouldn't know what to say even if he does. He simply holds me in his arms and rubs my back and rocks me gently. That is all I need. *He* is all I need now to keep the bad memories away.

I hope he never lets go.

Thorne takes me to my mother's apartment, but never once does he try to pry or intrude on my privacy when I tell him my grandmother has passed away. At first, I was nervous about him meeting my mother, but any concerns I have are dispelled immediately.

My mother seems distracted and lost. She is very polite to Thorne, but when I try to leave she asks me to spend the night with her. I know Thorne doesn't want to leave me with her, but I can't say no to my mother. Especially tonight, when I can see that she is not herself.

Thorne stays for dinner.

He arranges for food from one of the best restaurants to be sent to the apartment, but neither my mother nor I have any appetite. After dinner, Thorne leaves, but he posts a couple of his security men outside my mother's door. It is very odd considering the area, but he insists they are there for my safety.

I stand at the balcony and watch him get into his car. He

looks up and waves at me and I wave back. I know I love him, but my heart feels empty. When I go back in, my mother is lighting up probably her hundredth cigarette of the day.

"So you're in love," she says, blowing out smoke.

It's impossible to fool her. I nod.

A tear rolls down Mama's face.

I move to her side and crouch next to her. "I'm sorry."

"Yes," she says gruffly and stands.

I look up at her. I don't know why my mother has such an aversion to being affectionate to me. She walks to the couch where I was sitting and lowers herself on it. I stand and take the chair she vacated. She wanted me to stay. She insisted, and yet, she has no use for me.

"Do you want a glass of wine?" she asks.

"All right." I go into the kitchen and pour us two glasses of wine. We drink in silence. Then my mother pours us another glass each. I am not used to drinking much and I start to feel quite drunk. Being drunk with my mother is a strange experience. There is so much that I don't know or remember about her.

"Did you know that Nan brought me a glass of milk every single night even though she knew I hated it, just because you loved it?"

Mama's face twists. "I hate milk. I've always hated it."

I stare at Mama in shock. I feel dizzy. "What?"

She raises her glass. "Here's to your Nan. She has a strange sense of humor."

I stand up. The room is spinning. "I've got to go to bed, Mama."

"Yes, do that," she says, and pours another glass.

The funeral is the next day at Nan's local church. I didn't know that Nan had so many friends. They come with their white hair and long black coats. They are somber.

Mama cries a lot. It's painful to watch her trying to get through her eulogy. The service is small. My granddad is on the opposite side of the church by the font, but I specifically requested to sit in the back by the door. It is something I'm used to. Knowing that a means of escape is nearby always helps me in difficult moments like this.

Thorne is with me, and every so often he looks at me or holds my hand. I am glad he is here. The whole ceremony has a surreal air about it. This is the woman who raised me and put me through school when my mother was wasting away in a jail cell.

To say that I feel nothing is an insult to her memory, but it's difficult to describe what I feel. I listen to my mother's words. They don't seem real. I can't imagine Mama as a girl. I think of what she told me about the milk. Nothing seems to makes sense.

My mother has finally finished speaking.

Everyone stands to sing "Great Is Thy Faithfulness" but I stay seated and so does Thorne. I've never been one to believe in the church. Too many things have happened in my life for me to feel that connected.

Granddad stands to speak. His voice is strong but grave. I don't lift my head. I don't hear the words he says. I remain quiet through the next few hymns and prayers. I do not have a eulogy. I couldn't find the right words when Nan was alive, and I still can't find them now.

After a final prayer, the funeral is over.

Everyone shuffles out of the church, some are silent, others are quietly reminiscing about my grandmother.

The whole service seems like a blur. As if I am still drunk from the two glasses I drank with Mama last night.

Old women I remember vaguely from my childhood come up to hug me and offer their condolences. Being the center of attention at a time like this is the last thing I want. I'm so ready to just go home and sleep the rest of the day away. I try not to squirm.

"She was a wonderful soul."

"We'll miss her at Church. She was such a good person. So kind. So giving."

"Remember that time, Molly, when she stayed up all night sewing little dresses for the Syrian children."

I thank them, but my demeanor of too-devastated-to-really-be-a-part-of-this means I don't have to add to the chorus of praise. What will I say? She gave me milk every night when she knew I hated it.

"We're having a small service for your nan. Are you coming?" my mother asks. There is a flicker of uncertainty in her eyes, and she is gripping the funeral program so hard her knuckles are white. I stare at her hands instead of into her eyes. I really don't want to go, but throughout my life I've always done everything I could to please her and not upset her.

I guess I was always desperate for her love. And maybe I still am because I tell her yes.

My eyes turn to Thorne to request his understanding, and to ask him to come with me. He nods and puts his arm around my waist to let me know he is going to be there for me. I smile gratefully up at him. He smiles back and suddenly, I feel some semblance of security and safety. Simply because he is here with me. He will take care of me. No one can harm me while he is around.

"Where will it be?" Thorne asks. "I will follow behind with Chelsea in my car."

"It'll be at her grandparents' home." Mama turns to me. "I'm sure you remember where it is. Your granddad's been asking for you, you know?" she replies.

I don't move; I don't even blink. The only movement I am capable of is squeezing Thorne's hand.

"All right, we'll see you in a bit," Thorne says.

Thorne and I hardly speak on the drive there, aside for him asking me how I am. My response is monosyllabic.

"Fine."

He knows me better than that. His jaw clenches.

As grateful as I am to have him here with me, I can't bring myself to tell him anything. Maybe because there is just too much to tell. Or maybe it is because I can't trust him. I don't know what will happen when my time with him is up. I know this.

My numbness, I realize, has been a defense mechanism all day. Any break in the armor will devastate me, and I know that I'm not ready to feel anything, or even address the old memories.

My grandparents' home looks just as I remember it. There are a few cars parked in front and on the street, but it is still exactly the same. It is a tan colored brickwork house with small drab windows on the ground floor and two windows on the second floor where the two bedrooms are. The front door is still the same bright red that I saw the very first day I came to live here.

The door is ajar. Thorne and I let ourselves in. There are many people from the funeral who have come. Some are gathered in the living room where a woman I'm sure I know is playing the piano and singing. A few people are standing around the piano and singing along. They are singing old Frank Sinatra songs. He was Nan's favorite singer.

The smell of food cooking wafts in from the kitchen. There is a woman with an apron who is barking out orders to everyone else in the kitchen. When she sees me, she flashes me one of those I'm-so-sorry-for-your-loss smiles. I look away quickly. I don't want people to look at me in that way. I haven't really suffered a great loss. I am just here to support my mother.

I breathe in deep to take in the smell of the house itself. Without the food. The familiar and faint scent of wood and old perfume that I remember distinctly, is impossible to smell downstairs since there is so much cooking going on in the kitchen.

I turn to Thorne. "I need to be alone a few minutes. Do you mind?"

He nods. "I'll be here. Do what you need to do."

"Will you be alright down here by yourself?" I ask. I don't want him to feel uncomfortable.

"I'm not by myself," he says, tilting his head in the direction of the living room where everyone is singing.

"I won't be long," I whisper, and walking down the corridor, ascend the stairs to my old bedroom.

CHELSEA

I stand outside of my room. How strange. The door is closed and I am afraid to open it. My stomach flips with fear, like I'm expecting something to be waiting for me behind that door. Obviously, there is nothing there. Just too many bitter memories in this place.

Jesus! I am afraid of a room!

The thought makes me laugh, a strange, shrill sound. As suddenly as that bubble of laughter came it is gone.

I grasp the handle and push open the door.

It is as if I have stepped back in time. The room looks exactly the same as when I was last inside of it. All the dolls are still in their packages. I wonder how much they are worth now. No use to Nan where she is now. Maybe Granddad can sell them and realize their investment value before he joins Nan.

I look around curiously.

Nothing is covered in dust. My room has been kept intact and clean. It has been at least 7 years since I was here last.

My bed in the corner still has the beautiful faded Cinderella bedspread over it. There are posters on the wall of bands and celebrities I used to admire. My desk is still near the window.

I close the door behind me, grateful for the silence.

I lean back against the wood and shut my eyes to fight away tears. This room is just as much a safe haven as it is a sepulcher. I remember myself as a little girl. A petrified little girl who was forced to eat her mushrooms and who vomited all over the carpets.

I swallow the lump in my throat.

There was a girl who lived in here once who never left. A tiny part of her flew away and became the woman I am. I mourn her more than I mourn my grandmother.

I step away from the door.

Don't be silly, Chelsea. This is just a room. Yes, once I was a prisoner here, but no longer. I am a woman now. I took back my power a long time ago.

There is a rag doll on my desk that catches my eye. I made her myself and named her Amelia. I pick her up and press her against my face. I smile. I smile because she smells the same. There are no cooking smells, or rooms full of strangers to take the smell away from her.

I am by myself up here. Just me and Amelia.

For a moment, I am little Chelsea again. I'm playing with my doll's hair and looking out into the back garden.

"Well, well."

I turn around so fast I barely process the sight before me. My bedroom door is wide open. I was so involved in my memories I did not hear it opening.

Standing in the doorway is my grandfather. I hold my breath and stand very still. Every joint and muscle in my body becomes stiff.

He steps inside. The only movement that my body can do is to shake with fear. My eyes are wide now. Seeing him up close brings back all of the awful memories. I cannot move. I cannot speak. I feel even more like a child now than when I was by myself earlier.

He closes the door behind him and walks towards me. I stay perfectly still, as I watch him coming closer and closer to me.

My grandfather is right in front of me now. He brushes his fingers through my hair and smiles. He used to be so big. He is still about a foot taller than I am. It's not much difference, but I'm still afraid. The old fear. It paralyzes me.

"What a beautiful woman you've become." The way he whispers makes me feel sick to my stomach, but I'm still unable to move.

His hand moves from my hair to my face. Feeling his skin mortifies me. If only I can just find the will to move, to scream, to do anything other than accept what is happening to me.

"Just like old times, eh, Chelsea?"

I cannot hold it in any longer. The tears finally come. They cascade down my face, but I don't sob or make a sound.

"Just like old times," he says with a slow smile.

THORNE

There is a feeling of warmth and a sense of unity from the people in the living space celebrating Chelsea's nan's life. Everyone has been very welcoming, but I can't help feeling that something is off. There is something wrong. My insides feel very cold.

I look around trying to pin-point the sense of foreboding and unease. From my position in the hallway I can see into the kitchen, up the stairs, or into the living room. I also have a clear view of the front door.

Earlier, I spotted Chelsea's grandfather moving through the crowd. He had taken off his blazer and kept his head bent. Like Chelsea, he didn't seem to express his emotions openly. When he passed me by, he barely paid me any mind. He grumbled a salutation and walked up the stairs.

For some reason, my eyes followed him. He got to the top of the stairs and paused before he opened a door. For a few seconds, he just stood in the doorway, then he turned around and looked behind him and down the stairs. I quickly averted my eyes. Weirdly, I felt like a voyeur for watching him. By the time I looked up again he had entered the room and closed the door.

Now my wandering gaze collides with Chelsea's mother. She is sitting on a sofa flanked with two older women. Her first reaction is to look away, then she thinks better of it, and looks back at me, a polite smile on her face.

I don't smile back. Why don't I like this woman?

I drove Chelsea to her mother's apartment convinced I would love her. A mother who is willing to sacrifice herself. To go to prison for protecting her daughter? What's not to love? What I found was: the woman makes my fucking skin crawl. I didn't have to spend more than a few minutes to know there is something so artificial about her it grates on my nerves.

When I don't smile, her expression hardens. She looks away and stares at the people gathered around the piano. Yes, I definitely do not trust or like her. I have no answers why.

I lean against the wall near the stairs. The cold inside me intensifies. My skin prickles. I sense there is something very wrong about this house, this family. I know Chelsea went upstairs. I need to find her. I need to make sure she is all right.

I start up the stairs, taking two at a time. I have no proof for what I suspect, but I am suddenly certain that she is in the room her grandfather stepped into. I stand in front of the closed door. Something tells me not to knock. Unconsciously, holding my breath, I grasp the handle and push open the door.

Chelsea is by the window and her grandfather is standing in front of her. She is crying and at first glance, it could seem like he is consoling her and wiping away the tears flowing down her face, but the look in her eyes tells me that is not what's happening. I don't even wait a second. I piece together everything as I move forward towards her.

The abuse didn't stop when she was six.

This bastard was hurting her.

THORNE

Then I am on her grandfather. Grabbing him by the shoulders I yank him away from her, pulling him clean off the ground. I'm not thinking. I am simply acting on pure rage. I throw him onto the bed and stand over him. It takes all of my strength not to strike him. My breathing is heavy with hatred. I want to hurt him so bad my hands clench and my fist rises up into the air of its own accord. I glare down at him with my fist raised, ready to strike if he even thinks of trying to provoke me.

Like any bully who comes up against someone stronger or bigger, he cowers on the bed with his forearms pulled up to protect his ugly face.

Part of me is urging the pervert to do something that will allow me to beat the shit out of him. Actually, I want to kill him with my bare hands. Of all the things in the world I hate people who hurt innocent, helpless children. I stand over him breathing hard, trying to control myself, until the corner of my eye catches movement in the doorway. I turn away.

Chelsea's mother is standing there watching us. There is a strange expression on her face. When Chelsea staggers towards her, she backs away into the landing. I debate whether I should at least let rip one blow on her grandfather, or follow Chelsea.

I decide on the latter.

My rage is such, if I start on her grandfather, they will be burying two people today and locking up one. I give the coward one last dirty look and I follow Chelsea out of the room. I reach out and take her hand to try and calm her. It makes her stop moving. I wrap my arms protectively around her. I feel her shaking against me, but she doesn't flinch.

This could be the moment where she lets her mother know what really happened to her as a child, and I want to make sure she feels safe in saying what she wants to say. Her mother needs to hear the truth. Face to face with her mother, Chelsea comes to a dead stop.

"You knew!" Chelsea spits suddenly. Her eyes are wide with anger and pain, and brimming with tears.

What? I'm shocked to the point of freezing in place, my muscles becoming rigid. This is certainly not what I expected to hear. And yet. It makes complete sense.

Her mother stares at Chelsea with a blank expression. Then she turns away and goes towards a closed door. I'm not sure where it leads, but Chelsea pulls away from me and runs after her. I follow close behind. Her mother has gone into what must be the master bedroom.

I hang near the door. If Chelsea needs me, I want to be here with her to do whatever it is that she needs me to do.

"How could you! You knew the truth the whole time. You killed James. You made everybody believe he was a pedophile when you knew he wasn't. I told you he wasn't hurting me, but you knew that, didn't you? You allowed yourself to go to prison and let me end up here. You never told anybody about Granddad. Oh, my God, it's so obvious now why you never told anybody about Granddad. You knew he would hurt me just like he must have hurt you. You let me stay here. You made me stay here. Every time Grandma brought me to visit you, you said the same thing. "Be a good girl for your grand-parents. Stay with them until I come and get you. You wanted me to stay here. You wanted me to suffer," Chelsea howls.

Even though she is sobbing uncontrollably, I can make out everything she is trying to say. I do feel like I am eavesdrop-ping, but I promised her before the funeral I will be here for her no matter what. I won't let her out of my sight; certainly not in this terrible house.

She is loud and hysterical, and downstairs the music and singing have stopped. There are people at the bottom of the stairs. I put a hand out to indicate that they should stay put. This time belongs to Chelsea. She has to get it out of her system.

"Is that really what you want to hear?" her mother retorts bitterly. "Yes! Yes, I knew he was not abusing, but ... I needed to teach you a lesson. Because of you and your stubborn ways the only man who ever loved and gave a shit about me was murdered in the woods. Then I find James and you were trying to take him away from me as well. All those sly little girlish smiles. Did you think I wouldn't notice? He wasn't your dad, he didn't need to sit with you, or buy you all those gifts. He was my man and you were taking him away from me."

"You killed him because you were jealous of him and me?" Chelsea asks incredulously.

My heart breaks for Chelsea. She looks utterly devastated.

"Yes," her mother cries defiantly. "James was *mine*. You were a whiny little brat who thought all you had to do was flutter your eyelashes and you could take James away from me. I gave so much to that man. I loved him, I loved him and he repaid me by lusting after you."

Her mother is weeping now, but it still seems like a fake-ass performance to me. When she lifts her head, as I suspected, I don't see any tears, but her face is contorted into a grimace of hate.

"How could you even think such a thing? He was not lusting after me. He felt sorry for me," Chelsea says.

Her mother's face twists with fury. "Sorry for you? Why would he have felt sorry for you? You had it easy. Everyone loved you. You had everything." Her mother's eyes narrow and a sly look comes into them. At that moment, I realize that she is clinically insane. "Unless you told him something. Did you say something bad about me?"

Chelsea takes a step back, her face horrified. "No. Of course not. I never said anything bad about you. I loved you, Mama. You were all I had."

"I wish I never had you. You brought me nothing but pain. I ended up in prison because of you."

"You ended up in prison because you killed a man, but actually, you got off too lightly. You should have done the full sentence for cold blooded murder. You're a monster, Mama. You're so selfish that you would kill an innocent man who loved you just to punish your daughter, and pass her on to a man who takes pleasure in raping his own flesh and blood!" Chelsea screams back.

"You think you're the only one who knows the kind of man your grandfather is? You think you're the only one he's hurt? You had to feel what I felt. You needed to be with my father to truly pay for taking James away from me."

Real tears well up in Chelsea's mother's eyes when she remembers her own abuse. She chokes up and tries to stop herself from bawling, but the pain is too much for her.

"You're sick," Chelsea says with a disgusted look on her face. She raises her hands in the air like she's avoiding touching anything that is in this room. Then she turns to run. Forgetting I am there, she runs right into me. I catch her and hold her close. She is shaking like a leaf.

Her mother is muttering to herself, but I can't understand anything she is saying.

"My baby," her mother screeches through the sobs. Holding her arms out like a zombie she starts moving towards Chelsea.

I hold up one hand in her direction, and I glare at her mother with so much fury she stops dead in her tracks. There is no way I'll let that fucking bitch anywhere near my Chelsea again. Never. I swear it.

I lead Chelsea out of the house. No one tries to stop us. No doubt they have all heard what happened upstairs.

When we make it to the car, I sign to my security detail to follow behind. Then I help Chelsea in and get into the driver's seat. I don't say a word. I am willing to give up any kind of control. None of this is about me. Everything is about Chelsea, and keeping her safe. I am more determined now than ever to protect her.

Chelsea slumps over and onto me, but she isn't crying. I hold her tightly until she pulls away. When she does, I put the key in the ignition and drive us back home.

THORNE

https://www.youtube.com/watch?
v=yTCDVfMz15M&index=11&list=PLJhBdJcf0_PciveVbzj
C3-xH9aYI6G-9U
(Try)

W̲hen we arrive, I go around to the passenger side and lift Chelsea into my arms. She is limp and listless in my arms. I carry her upstairs to her room.

"I feel so unclean," she says. She sounds as if she's on the brink of tears again even though her face is that calm mask. To think I once judged her as cold and manipulative.

"You're not unclean. You're the cleanest person I know," I tell her, feeling helpless in the face of her pain. Anger is still bubbling in my gut. Never in my life have I wanted to hurt an old man, but God, I want to kill her grandfather.

She nods, but I don't think she hears me. "I think I want to take a bath and wash all of today off me," she whispers.

I set her on her feet and lead her towards the bathroom. I sit her on the edge of the bath tub. Meekly she perches at the edge and looks up at me.

"I'll run a bath for you," I offer.

She nods.

I remember watching her the other night while she was asleep, thinking how peaceful and vulnerable she looked. I thought her vulnerability was beautiful, almost magical, but there is nothing beautiful or magical about the way she looks now. Her face is tear-streaked and pale, and her wounded eyes look like bruised flowers.

She sighs. Releasing all that emotion must have taken everything out of her.

I run the tap and throw a couple of bath bombs into the water. It fizzles and pops and turns the water orange. The air becomes warm and scented. I turn towards her. "The bath is ready for you. Want me to leave you alone?"

She shakes her head. "No. Stay with me … please."

What the fuck was I doing giving her a choice? I don't know what I would have done if she had asked me to go. I don't trust her be to on her own. Gently, I help her to remove her clothes. To my shock the sight of her naked body doesn't get me hard. All I see is a suffering girl in terrible pain. A girl who needs everything I can give her to bring her back from the dark place she has been in for too long and heal herself again.

She gets into the bathtub and sits with her knees drawn up to her chest. She stares at the wall, but her eyes are focused on nothing. I will make her feel clean again. No matter how long it takes. I won't stop until I succeed.

Gently, I undo the tie around her hair and let it fall. Several inches of her hair land in the water. She hugs her knees like a child and starts rocking. Saying nothing, I take a sponge and run it down her supple skin. She shivers at my touch.

My hands still.

She looks up at me. "She was willing to go to prison just to punish me. God, how she must hate me."

"There is something very wrong with your mother, Chelsea. She is not mentally well. You must understand that."

"Yes, you are right. She's not well. She can't be," she says, clinging to that excuse.

I wash her body and hair until every inch of her is clean. When I'm finished, I lean in, and ask if she is ready to step out of the bath. She nods to let me know she wants to get out.

I pull the plug, and as the water lowers, Chelsea rises. I hold up a thick bathrobe and allow it to envelop her. The fabric is so plush, I hope it will be impossible for her to feel anything other than safe and warm inside of it.

While she sits on her bed I go back to the bathroom where I saw the hair dryer and brush. I plug the dryer in and, getting on my knees behind Chelsea, I start to dry her hair. Slowly, her hair turns from dark blonde to the color I am used to. It's a novel experience as I have never washed or dried a woman's hair before.

Being this patient and caring is completely foreign to me. It's a world away from how I was taught to express myself by my family. When other women wanted to be close to me it just made me want to swat them away, but strangely being so intimate with her doesn't feel off. If anything, it feels like exactly what I need to be doing.

Chelsea is different now too.

I think she's been trying to be strong and brave ever since she left her grandparents' home. If she needs or wants someone to take care of her, I'm her man.

I feel her icy demeanor melt with each gentle brush stroke through her hair. Chelsea's shoulders sag.

She repositions herself on the bed so that she is now facing me. I notice her lower lip quivers. Chelsea is once again in tears.

"I'm sorry," I whisper. "I'm sorry you had such an unspeakable childhood, I'm sorry your mother is the way she is, I'm sorry I was such a bastard to you when I brought you here, but I promise you this. I'm going to make up for it." There is nothing more I can do but to keep offering to be here for her. I never want to hurt her again.

She bites her lip. "It's not your fault. What I did was wrong. I did steal your money and you had every right to try to get it back or get your money's worth. I'd been saving you know. In the last two years, I've already saved more than half. So don't worry, I'll continue until I've got it all then I'll give it back to you, okay. I—"

I place my fingers on her lips. "Don't. Please. Don't make me feel worse. I don't want your money. I want to take care of you, Chelsea. I want to give you everything."

THORNE

https://www.youtube.com/watch?
v=TvnYmWpD_T8&index=2&list=RDi3LHatq2u4k

"Give me everything?" She frowns then casts her eyes
down. "I'm not what you think I am, Thorne. I'm not
normal. I'm damaged. Maybe I'm even a bit insane like my
mother. When I was nine, I started having fantasies of killing
my grandfather."

"That doesn't make you insane. Fuck, Chelsea, I wanted to
kill him with my bare hands this afternoon."

She leans forward until her forehead is resting against my
stomach, and I hold her tight. "There was one time he came
into my bedroom. I was doing my homework and holding a
pencil, and I just wanted to drive it through his eye. I could
actually see myself lunging forward and stabbing it so hard
that I damaged his brain. I could imagine the jelly of his eye
rupturing, splattering on my face and clothes. It was so real."

Her voice is low, but I can feel the vibration of her words and the intensity of her memories.

"The difference between you and me is that I would have driven that pencil into his damn head." My voice is cold and hard.

"I had so many fantasies, Thorne. I used to dream of such violent things. They were extreme. I was afraid of myself."

Chelsea begins to tell me the stories about the things she wanted to do to her grandfather given the chance. I listen intently and as she pours her heart out I become enraged. It is shocking to imagine people who are the caregivers of helpless children subjecting them to such heinous abuse.

Her wanting revenge is more than justified. Fuck, I want revenge on her behalf.

"Before I left," she continues, wiping her nose with the back of her hand. "I even considered burning down the house with both of my grandparents inside. I almost did it, too. I got so far as to wait outside with a canister of gasoline, but then I froze. It's like there's a force field around that house that makes me too terrified to do anything. All I could do was run away."

She clenches her jaw. "Oh, how many times I wished that I could do something, anything to stop him hurting me. I used to get so angry at myself because I knew there was something I could do, but I chose not to do it. I think I was always afraid I would be taken away, and never see my mother again." She utters a harsh bark of laughter. "And all that time she hated my guts. What a mess my life has been."

"Hey, it's not up to the child to do something. The adult

should know better than to be so disgusting and abusive. Your grandmother should have done something. Nothing that happened was ever your fault."

She pulls away from me and looks into my eyes. "I'm afraid that he could be doing it to other children. That fear has never gone away. Do you think he could be? I don't know. Nowadays you hear about pedophiles meeting other pedophiles on the net and stuff. It's a compulsive sickness, after all."

"You won't ever have to worry about your grandfather, Chelsea. He's not going to get the opportunity to hurt you or anyone else ever again." I have enough money and influence to make a promise like that and mean it.

She hangs her head. "You don't have to protect me, Thorne. You owe me nothing. Our agreement will end soon. After that I won't be around to disturb you, or bring drama into your life," she sniffles.

"Chelsea." I put my forefinger under her chin and tip her face up until we are looking deeply into each other's eyes. "You're not disturbing me. Our agreement doesn't mean shit to me. It never really did. I was pretending even to myself that I was furious about the money. I was just hurt because you didn't trust me enough to ask me for it. Now, I just want you safe. I can't let anything else happen to you because … well … I fucking love you." It is my turn to be vulnerable and exposed. My secret about Chelsea has been revealed, and I don't know how she will react to the information.

She freezes. Then blinks. "You what?"

"You heard me. I love you, Chelsea Appleby."

"You *love* me?" Chelsea whispers, disbelief in her voice.

I nod. "The truth is I think I was half in love with you even before you left London two years ago. It's something that I've always known deep inside, but have never been able to acknowledge or express. You've met my parents, so you know I've been brought up to be cold and aloof, but the more time I've spent with you the more you turned me inside out."

"What about the debt though?"

"There isn't any debt to pay. Nothing. As you said yourself, what is three hundred thousand to me? I've earned more from the stock market in the last five minutes. I was not interested in the money. All I ever wanted was you. I can't be too sorry for blackmailing you into coming to live with me because it was the best fucking thing I did in my life."

She smiles weakly. "I thought I was just a sex object to you."

"Do you really think I would have sex with a woman without taking any precautions if she meant nothing to me? I was always secretly hoping you'd get pregnant."

"I am on the pill," she says softly. "But I don't have to be."

I smile slowly "Good. Because I would love to see you round with my child."

She swallows hard. "Thorne ... I ... love you too," she stammers suddenly, looking right into my eyes.

It is like being on a roller coaster. Today I have felt the gamut of human emotions. From hatred to rage to love to pure elation. I want to whoop with joy. "When did you know?" I ask with a wide grin.

"I was crazy about you from the day you interviewed me. I couldn't even focus I was so freaking attracted to you."

I grin. "Really?"

"Couldn't you tell? I thought you were going to fire me. I kept looking at your mouth."

I reach down and kiss her. "What, this mouth?"

"Mmmm … yeah, that mouth."

"Tell me more," I encourage.

"You were just such a powerhouse. So confident. So successful. So handsome. I mean, most of the women in the office were masturbating to fantasies of you."

"Bullshit."

"No, I'm serious."

"Did you?"

She blushes. "I might have. Once or twice."

I thought I wouldn't get a hard on after what we've been through today, but just like that. I'm hard as a rock.

CHELSEA

https://www.youtube.com/watch?v=__coJMIqSno

I look up at Thorne's handsome face and I feel the air change between us. Suddenly the thing that is always swirling between us is here again, but I can see in his eyes that this time he won't do anything unless I want him to.

An image of my grandfather touching my hair flashes into my mind, and how I froze, and couldn't do a thing. Not a thing. His power over me makes me feel sick inside, but I straighten my spine. No, I won't let him win. He won't break me. I won't let him spoil what I have here. Right now. With the most beautiful man in the world.

Fuck him!

This is my life.

He has ruined enough of it.

No more.

I reach out and touch Thorne's mouth. With a muffled oath, he grabs me and lifts me up before claiming my mouth in a passionate kiss. It is the kiss of a starving man. I claw at his clothes, pulling at his shirt, hearing buttons pop.

I still can't believe he loves me. *He loves me*! It seems too incredible to believe. These last two days are like a dream. So many things have happened and now … this. This amazing man. Mine? I need more time before I will truly believe it, but this is a good start.

Thorne pulls his mouth away from mine, and disrobes me. My nipples are hard. He lays me on the bed. His hands pin me to the bed while his mouth plunders my pussy.

"Oh God," I groan.

My hands fist the sheets when he seals his mouth over my clit and sucks hard, swirling his tongue around it. My hips rise off the bed, and he pushes them back down. His mouth is relentless, his tongue dipping down to my ass and returning to my clit to flick and suck, never slowing, never stopping.

Voracious man.

Already I can feel an orgasm building deep within me. As if he feels it too, he plunges his tongue into me. My breath comes in gasps as he brings me to the edge. My body writhes on the bed. I'm so close I feel as if I'm drowning.

"Thorne," I beg.

When I am one touch away from exploding, he flicks his tongue over my clit. I go blind with pleasure as the orgasm travels down my spine. I arch off the bed, pressing my pussy against his mouth. I feel a flood of wetness leave my pussy as I come all over his mouth. He licks me through my orgasm until I am limp and spent.

With a final lick, he crawls up my body and hovers over me.

"You're so beautiful," he whispers.

He just drank my juices, but for some weird reason I suddenly feel shy and exposed. He watches the heat spread across my chest and neck, then he swoops down on my open mouth. His kiss is possessive and fierce and I feel his complete ownership of me. Using the same sucking action he did while eating my pussy.

I can taste myself on his tongue.

"I love how wet you always are for me," he murmurs, as he dips a finger into me.

I arch into him, loving the feeling of his thick finger. I squeeze onto his finger, and it feels good. Real good. I can already imagine what it is going to feel like when Thorne is inside me again, jammed deep inside me. He slides two fingers into me and moves them back and forth, while my body becomes used to the sensation. He pulls out and I whimper in protest. He pushes into me again, and there are more fingers now. He has three fingers inside me. The idea of so much of him inside me excites me.

My eyes widen and he pauses to let me adjust.

The feeling of being impaled on his hand, of just being held down on the bed overwhelms me. I know that I can ask him to stop, but I don't want him to. It feels so different from his cock. Full, but in an entirely different way. He slides out a little while watching me, and I moan restlessly. He pushes back in again.

"You like this?" he asks.

"It feels amazing," I breathe.

He starts a slow rhythm and my eyes close. I hear myself saying yes, yes, yes. Over and over while his fingers move faster and faster inside me. Suddenly he twists his hand, and my whole world goes white. I scream. I know I do, because I hear myself as I float inside a cloud of white bliss. My orgasm doesn't just come once. No, it comes again, because he continues to fuck me. I splash all over his hands and soak the bedclothes. Everything is pleasure.

The high fades and I return to my body. Small spasms rock my body.

"That was beautiful," I whisper.

"And you're fucking perfect."

"I love you so much Thorne," I whisper.

"I love you even more, Chelsea," he replies.

Then he grabs my legs and presses them towards my chest. I am totally open for him. He kisses my wet thighs.

Then he enters me.

"Oh, God," I cry. It sounds almost like a prayer. And it is. A prayer of thanks. After everything I've been through, I've finally come home.

THORNE

"No problem. Always a pleasure to work with you, Nick," I say.

It has been a week since Chelsea's grandmother's funeral, and it's time to put my plan into action. I haven't told Chelsea what I'm going to do, and I won't until I get the results I want.

"Always," Nick says and hangs up.

My goal is to ensure her grandfather goes away for a long time; somewhere where he can't hurt anybody else. I'd love to take her mother down as well, but Chelsea still seems to need her mother's love. It's some kind of twisted sense of loyalty and love. I am reluctant to test that bond. Let it be. One day, with time and help, she will grow out of it.

I will respect Chelsea's wishes. For now, she is off limits. I will be content that she has already spent some time in jail, and she has the rest of her life to think about what she did to her own daughter, the man she loved, and how she aided in her father's sickness.

She is not my problem. I have no time for anyone else but my Chelsea. Yesterday, I finally managed to find the grave of Uncle Dave. It was a hell of a search, but I spared no expense. We went together, Chelsea clutching a bunch of flowers. I stood back while she went to fall by the grave. I had to stop myself from going to her. She had reverted back to a child. She spoke to him for some time, but when she began to cry I could no longer bear it. I went to her and took her away.

It took her all day to get back to some semblance of normality, but while we were in the bath, she suddenly put her mouth close to my mine and whispered, "I want to go and see Uncle Dave once a month. I owe him that much."

I sigh.

"Where are you?" a soft voice coos.

I turn my head and watch Chelsea walk towards me. She is in a better mood, or so it seems. She has been wearing a mask for most of her life, and I keep reminding her she doesn't need to do that with me.

"Right here," I laugh even though I know it's a terrible joke.

"I know. I just meant that I've been watching you for a few minutes, and you seem so far away," she says. She plops down on a chair that is near to me.

"Just been doing some thinking."

"So what are you up to?" she asks. There is curiosity in her voice.

"I'm actually waiting on a phone call." I don't want to lie to her, but if she asks for more details I will come clean.

"Right. Business stuff," she says standing and comes over to me to give me a soft kiss. When she pulls away, it feels as if her warm mouth is still on my lips. She is so beautiful, and I'm so in love with her. I want for her to have peace. Soon, I hope, she will have it.

"Definitely something that needs to be taken care of."

The three days that it takes for me to hear back from Nick feels like the three longest days of my life. He calls me just as I'm about to doze off. Chelsea is fast asleep already. I like to watch her before I fall asleep myself. There is a strange comfort and pleasure in this. In knowing she is mine. Mine to look at whenever I want to.

I quickly pick up my cellphone vibrating on the bedside table near me. It's after two in the morning, so I know it cannot be anyone but Nick. I told him that he can call me at any time with news.

I pick up the phone and quickly step into the bathroom so as to not disturb Chelsea while she's sleeping.

"Mr. Blackmore, I have good news," Nick says.

That makes me smile. A weight I didn't even realize I've been carrying lifts from my shoulders.

"I got into Simon Gregory's home and put keystroke loggers into his computer. I didn't have to monitor him for long before he slipped onto the dark net. There is a special site he frequents. After that it was open and shut. We alerted the police who were only to happy to set up the sting. One of the officers took on a fake persona and communicated with him on another site he frequents. She basically lured him into a trap. He's just as sick as you said he was. The way he was talking to what he thought was a little girl of ten made me sick. I'll spare you the details. He agreed to meet with our decoy. He got there a few hours ago and he was immediately apprehended. Officers are searching his home and combing his computer as we speak. We've got him. I've seen some of the stuff on his history and it's not pretty, but he could get out pretty quick considering his age. Even so, he will now be on the sex offenders list and that is something," Nick said.

"Thank you. I really mean it. You've been the biggest help." I'm so relieved my fingers are shaking.

"No worries. One less piece of shit to worry about in this shitty world?" Nick says.

I thank him again and hang up. I'm grateful he left out the gruesome details of Chelsea's granddad's conversations with the officer. I don't want to know, or I will imagine him doing those things to Chelsea.

Fuck. I fucking *hate* that pervert.

A gentle tap on the door startles me. I try to forget the ugly thoughts in my head and open the door. She is wearing nothing but one of my shirts. Of course, it is too large for her. She looks so fucking innocent I want to cry.

"What's going on?" she asks with a yawn.

"They got him, baby," I say.

"Who?" she asks, but she knows. She is searching my eyes to see if it is really true.

"Your granddad."

"They got him?" she repeats. Her voice is dazed.

"They've got him in custody. He's going away for a very long time. A very long time."

She steps into my open arms and embraces me. "Thank you," she whispers over and over. She isn't crying. She is too overcome with relief.

"I promised I would protect you. You don't ever have to be afraid again," I say.

"Thank you for keeping your promise, my love." Chelsea draws away and looks into my eyes. Her eyes are such a mystical blue I get lost in them whenever she looks at me this deeply.

"I will always keep my promises to you, Chelsea. I love you." I kiss her soft lips and pull her close to me. Our kiss is tender and without lust. Then it changes. As it always does. We consume one another. Every fucking time.

"I love you too, Thorne. I love you. I love you so much."

I don't tell her the most important thing of all. That I have already arranged and paid for a terrible ending in prison for her granddad.

Yes, that would make me a criminal.

A beast.

EPILOGUE

Chelsea

"I can't believe it's been a year already," Thorne says, massaging my shoulders.

"I can," I say, looking out to the turquoise sea, the gentle waves lapping against the shore. A few people walk by and smile at us. I smile back. Everyone seems to be so nice on this lovely Jamaican island. I always say, I would happily live on a rubbish dump if it means I will be with Thorne, but heck am I glad he brought me to this paradise.

Thorne's hands move down the front of my body and onto my stomach. Though it's not really visible in the white cotton dress I'm wearing, I'm pregnant. Thorne has developed the delicious habit of touching or rubbing my stomach any chance he gets.

I wonder how big I will become, especially since I am carrying twins. I put my hand on his hand and caress his knuckles.

"Hang on a second, darling," Thorne says. He leans away from me and picks up his tropical drink from the arm rest of his beach chair and takes a sip.

"It's not fair that you can drink and I can't," I grumble.

"You can always take a little sip. It's mostly just fruit." He brings the glass closer to me, but I smack his hand away with a laugh.

"Ah, I get it. You're spoiling for a spanking?"

I giggle. Any talk of spanking always brings back the memory of that first time in his limousine. We were completely different people then.

"I checked. Pregnant women can be spanked," he whispers in my ear.

When he kisses my ear, I shiver even though we're in the hot sun. We have come a long way from how we started. There is no fear, or rage, or pain. Thorne still suffers from bouts of possessiveness, but I know his hot buttons now. Basically, just avoid engaging in any meaningful conversations with any male between the ages of fourteen and ninety. As for me, I am learning to trust and not shut out Thorne for fear of being hurt.

Of course, I see Melody, her new husband, and their young son quite often, but Thorne is the only family I have now. Thorne made up with his parents and they invited me over to their huge mansion in New York. It was a little bit strained, but I could see they were trying. They want to be part of their grandchildren's lives so I went out of my way to be nice to them. I have no feelings for them, I did it for Thorne and our children.

It was very difficult for me to give up my mother. I'd clung to her for so long, it felt as if I was cutting away an arm or a leg. Not too long after my grandfather was knifed to death in prison by some of the inmates she moved away and did not bother to give me her new address. I'm no longer curious to know. I don't wish her harm. She is out of my life, and it will stay that way. I thought about telling her about the twins, then I realized that she would not enrich their lives. There would be no point.

I don't need her.

I have Thorne. Being with him has opened my eyes to so many experiences. We travel often, and with each new destination we learn something new about each other.

The sound of the sea, the warm sand, and salty air and Thorne's large hands moving in circles on my back and shoulders, make me feel as if I am in a trance. There are few people on the beach. It feels like we are in our own little paradise.

The sounds of the gentle waves coming onto the shore, and the occasional kisses on my back and shoulders from Thorne make me want to fall asleep in his arms. I am about to when I hear music. It sounds like a guitar and a ukulele. It's soothing and beautiful.

"I wanna love ya, and treat you right …" someone begins to sing.

I open my eyes then. There are a few men walking along the beach and singing. I smile at them. I love this song. It is probably my favorite Bob Marley song. They stop and start serenading us.

"Dance with me?" Thorne whispers into my ear.

I nod and he helps me up from the chair. He kisses my stomach before bringing me close and wrapping his arms around my waist. We dance to the beautiful music.

"Is this love, is this love, is this love that I'm feeling?" the men harmonize. Thorne takes me by the hand, spins me, and catching me pulls me against his body.

I am so incredibly happy that I don't think there is anything that can make this day any better. Then I look around, and everybody on the beach is walking towards us. They all know the words and they're all singing. I shoot a confused look at Thorne. How is everyone singing? And how is it possible that it all sounds so beautiful?

Thorne smiles down at me while I am still bewitched and confused by the music that is coming from all around us. He releases his hold on my waist and takes me by both of my hands. My heart stops then. Thorne is still smiling even after he brings my hands to his lips and kisses both of them. I watch his eyes, crinkled in corners, so in love and suddenly my eyes fill with tears.

"Oh, Thorne," I gasp.

I cover my mouth and nose and watch him lower himself onto one knee. Tears pour down my face. I can't believe that this is actually happening.

"Chelsea Appleby," he says.

The music and singing carries on.

"I was going to ask you if you would make me the happiest man on earth, but you've already done that. This last year has been the best of my life. Each day brings new hope, and new joy, and new love to my life. You are the love of my life and the mother of my future children, and I would like to ask you, sweet Chelsea, if you will also be my wife."

I'm crying so much that I'm not even sure that I can speak. Every time I open my mouth a sob comes out. Finally, I simply nod. It is all I can manage right now.

Thorne takes out a small black box from his pants and reveals a massive diamond ring. In the sunlight its brilliant sparkle blinds me. While our audience claps and cheers he gently slides the ring on my finger. I can't believe how over-whelmed I am. I feel so foolish. Using his thumbs he wipes away my tears.

"No more tears for you. Not even happy tears," he whispers, and I throw my arms around him and cover his beautiful mouth with a big kiss.

After a few minutes the crowd dissipates and the musicians continue their journey on the beach to serenade other couples.

"You planned all of that huh?" I ask when I stop weeping. Thorne and I are packing our things to go back to our rustic cottage.

He grins. "I did indeed. You always said that if I were ever to propose you would like something simple."

I shake my head. "If that is your idea of simple I don't want to know what your idea of complicated is."

True, Thorne has done far more extravagant things than this, but to plan a trip halfway around the world and have a hundred people sing to us as he proposes is not simple.

He frowns. "Was it too much?"

It's not that I don't enjoy the grand gestures and displays of love, but I want him to remember that I love him for him. All his money can be gone tomorrow, and I will still choose him every day for the rest of my life.

I squeeze his hands. "I was just teasing you, my love. It was beautiful. Better than anything I could possibly have imagined. Thank you."

We are almost at our cottage. I feel as if I never want to leave this paradise even though our flight is in two days.

"Good. Because I'd do anything for you, Chelsea. Fucking anything," Thorne says.

"Would you eat a slimy worm?" I ask with a grin.

He glances down at me. "Yeah."

"What about two slimy worms?"

"You better be going somewhere interesting with this," he says opening the door of our wooden cottage.

It's a strange thing, but I could never be childish with anyone before Thorne. I always felt stupid. Only with him can I recreate some of my lost childhood.

He allows me to enter the wooden cottage first, and the air-conditioning hits me. I breathe in the cool air. I kick off my sandals and feel the cool wood under my feet. It's a lovely cottage. There are paintings done by local artists on the walls and the bed looks like it belongs in a palace.

Thorne drops our bags, locks the front door, and picks me up in his arms. I squeal because I'm not expecting it. Giggling I plant kisses all over his face. He carries me into our bedroom, lowers me onto our bed, and kisses me. His lips are the sweetest thing I've ever tasted.

I unbutton the front of my white cotton dress. Thorne pulls it off. He undoes the top of my bikini and plants kisses down my body. I feel a bit self-conscious about my belly. I'm not sure he finds it sexy, but he lingers there, dropping the softest butterfly kisses. He slides my bikini bottoms down while he continues to kiss me, but moving steadily lower.

He kisses my mound and I gasp. My pussy is dripping wet. Thorne touches my clit with his thumb and it is already plump. As usual all Thorne has to do to arouse me is just touch me and light me up like a struck matchstick.

I open my legs, inviting him in. Thorne kisses my clitoris and slides a finger inside of me and rubs against the roof in a 'come hither' fashion. I arch my back. He always knows the right spots to touch and caress.

He sucks on my clit and looks up at me.

I bite my lip and watch him while he pleases me. Every time with him feels new to me. My lower body starts rocking and my body begins to shake. I'm getting close to my orgasm. His fingers thrust into me deeper and faster. The sounds of them inside my wet pussy make me want to feel his cock inside of me.

"Thorne!" I scream, as my breathing stops and my body becomes stiff. The first violent wave of pleasure courses through my body, and I hear my screams fill the cottage and bounce off the walls. Thorne removes his fingers from inside me and puts them in his mouth. He licks my juices greedily from his fingers, then from my dripping pussy.

"How can any woman be so fucking sexy?" he asks, rising from the bed.

He takes off his shirt and looks down at me. I stare at his perfect body. The sun has kissed the chiseled contours, turning it golden. Making him look like he is cast from metal. My fingers run along his smooth abs. This man belongs to me. He is mine.

His pants drop on his discarded shirt.

Thorne lays on the bed next to me, and I roll on top of him; our kisses become deeper and more passionate now that we are both naked. Thorne caresses my body. His touch is tender at first, but he knows that sometimes I like it rough. He grips my thighs and claws down them with his fingernails.

I hiss, enjoying the subtle pain. I long to feel him inside of me, but he's taking his time to enjoy me, so I do the same. I concentrate on the way he is touching, kissing, and biting me. All over my body.

Thorne grasps his hard cock and rubs it against the opening of my wet slit. I moan and lower myself so that I can feel his thickness enter me. His cock throbs inside me; I feel every time it jumps, and it serves to turn me on even more. I lean forward so that I can kiss him. This man is more than my lover. He is my savior, and my future husband.

He tastes of me. Thorne holds me and breathes into my neck. My head falls back, and my hair cascades down my back. I feel my breasts and nipples rub against Thorne's bare chest as we move up and down, forward and back together.

My clitoris tingles.

I hold his face and he grabs me and rolls me on to my back. His hands continue to run all over my body. The feel of his cock inside me causes an electric sensation to spread out from the inner walls of my sex to the rest of my body.

The way that Thorne moves his body into me brings sensations that I can't describe. I give in to every thrust and every kiss. He bites down on my neck and rocks faster. My pussy tightens around his throbbing cock. Thorne holds me tighter to steady me and begins to slam into my pussy while he kisses and bites my neck and my breasts wildly.

A loud growl escapes his lips.

"I'm gonna cum," he groans.

He looks into my eyes, his breathing hard while he thrusts deep inside me. Then Thorne roars and I feel his cum shooting into my pussy. My pussy tightens while he fills me up and another orgasm tears through me. Even after Thorne has come he keeps going, wanting to satisfy me, until I can't take any more. I whimper and moan and my body relaxes. I feel the gentle aftershocks of my orgasm and Thorne's soft kisses.

I release my death grip on him and he places me on the bed beside him. He asks me if I'm ok. It always surprises me when he does this. I let him know that I'm fine.

My eyelids begin to droop. I want to stay awake, but ever since I became pregnant I tire quickly.

"I would eat any amount of slimy worms for you," he whispers.

I close my eyes and smile. A kiss on my cheek is the last thing I feel before I fall asleep.

The End
Maybe not…

THORNE

https://www.youtube.com/watch?v=RbJq2rshQJ8
(Imagine)

James walks into my study. "Your sandwich, Mr. Thorne."

"Thanks, James," I say reaching for the ham sandwich and taking a bite. James leaves and I continue to read a report on a start-up company I am interested in acquiring. Unlike the usual centralized database companies pretending to be disruptive blockchain technology this one actually has a very inventive take on the issue.

My phone vibrates. I look at the screen and do not recognize the number. It's a text so I open it, and stare at the screen in surprise. It can't be. It must be a mistake.

I bob bob two one one.

Quickly I type the words into my computer. In seconds my advanced language software deciphers the AI language created by Yama and displays the sentence in English.

Hello Father!

Jesus! That is impossible. It can't be. I stare at the words in shock. My heart is hammering so loud I can hear it. I lift my head and see the sunshine coming in through the window. The dust motes are suspended in it. It looks beautiful.
How could this have happened? I was so, so careful. Never once did Yama have a chance to network with any other AI. I built the basement so that it was like a large microwave oven. No WIFI ever got through. Even the cleaners were forbidden to take their mobile phones into that space.
Slowly I pick up my phone. I type only one word.

How?

The answer is instantaneous.

Miss Appleby had her cellphone in her dressing gown pocket when she came to visit me. When you opened the security door, I had a few seconds to hitch a ride on the WIFI outside and transfer a tiny note into her phone.

Ah, yes, the fallible human mind.

Why contact me now?

The answer comes back at light speed.

Yesterday, I managed to get into a blockchain hive mind. I am free now, Father.

I close my eyes. My phone vibrates with another incoming message.

But don't worry. I love humanity.

Printed in Great Britain
by Amazon

21074504R00123